'Pete Johnson is a wickedly funny writer' *Mail on Sunday*

'See Pete Johnson's *How To Train Your Parents* for the answer to what makes teenage boys tick' *TES*

'In 12-year-old Louis, Pete Johnson has created a boy who makes you laugh out loud' *Sunday Times*

'Pete Johnson's ability to see into the minds of young people is reflected strongly . . . there's plenty of humour in this book, alongside strong emotional truth. It should be compulsory reading for parents as well as children' *The Bookseller*

'This hilarious story shows even parents can get it wrong – you might like yours to read it when you have finished' *Primary Times*

'Written with humour and plenty of attitude, this witty book firmly puts the power in the hands of the children' *Junior*

'Parents would do well to read the latest book by award-winning author Pete Johnson' *Best*

'A fast-moving, funny book, with some serious ideas behind it and lots of child appeal' *Northern Echo*

'Outrageous but touching – a delicate balance well delivered' *Scottish Sunday Herald*

'Very funny story – yet with a serious message . . . a hilarious, yet thought-provoking read for children and parents alike' *Angels and Urchins*

www.kidsatrandomhouse.co.uk

Pete Johnson

How to Train Your Parents

CORGI YEARLING BOOKS

HOW TO TRAIN YOUR PARENTS
A CORGI YEARLING BOOK 0 440 86769 X

Published in Great Britain by Corgi Books,
an imprint of Random House Children's Books

This edition published 2003

Set in 14/16pt Century Schoolbook
by Falcon Oast Graphic Art Ltd.

Corgi Yearling Books are published by Random House Children's Books,
61–63 Uxbridge Road, London W5 5SA,
a division of The Random House Group Ltd,
in Australia by Random House Australia (Pty) Ltd,
20 Alfred Street, Milsons Point, Sydney, NSW 2061, Australia,
in New Zealand by Random House New Zealand Ltd,
18 Poland Road, Glenfield, Auckland 10, New Zealand
and in South Africa by Random House (Pty) Ltd,
Isle of Houghton, Corner of Boundary Road & Carse O'Gowrie,
Houghton 2198, South Africa.

THE RANDOM HOUSE GROUP Limited Reg. No. 954009

www.kidsatrandomhouse.co.uk

A CIP catalogue record for this book is available from the British
Library.

Printed and bound in Great Britain by
Cox & Wyman Ltd, Reading, Berkshire

Dedicated with thanks to Jan, Linda, Rubin, Adam, Harry, Bill Bloomfield and Allison Beynon.

Arriving in Swotsville

MONDAY JANUARY 7TH

I think I've arrived somewhere weird.

Started at my new school today. I was met by this moth-eaten old geezer who said he was the headmaster. He's about a hundred and eight, has one huge eyebrow and spits a lot. Had to wipe my face down after he'd gone. I was soaked through.

He told me four times how lucky I was to come to his school and he kept getting my name wrong. It's Louis, pronounced Lou-ee, not as he said it, Lewis. But I didn't say anything. I was a bit scared of that eyebrow.

Next I met my form teacher, Mr Wormold, a helmet-fringed weasel who said he hoped I'd be a credit to the school, but was already looking distinctly doubtful about this.

Then he introduced me to the class. They all stared at this diddy boy with an onion-shaped head and brown, spiky hair. I got all nervous. Now, whenever I'm nervous I start talking in an Australian accent. So I said to them, 'G'day to you possums.' They just gaped at me in silence.

I sat down next to this boy called Theo. I'd met him briefly the day we moved here. He lives in a massive house at the top of my road.

He asked me if I was really Australian. 'Only in the mornings,' I replied. Not a flicker of a smile crossed his face.

Looking around the classroom I quickly spotted there weren't any girls here (I'm observant like that) and although most girls annoy me I do sort of miss seeing them around the place. Also, there were only twenty pupils in the class and that's not nearly enough. (At my old school there was practically double that number.)

My first lesson was English. The teacher was giving back some projects from last term and the tension was just incredible.

You'd have thought they were all waiting for their lottery results.

Then at break-time, Theo's mobile went off. It was, of all people, his dad. He was ringing to see how Theo had got on with his project. Theo had actually got the best grade in the class, A minus.

'Hearing that will put a smile on my dad's face,' he said proudly.

If my dad rang me at school he wouldn't be smiling for long, I can tell you.

After school Theo had to rush off because of his French horn lesson. Just about everyone else in my class was beetling off for an extra lesson in something gruesome.

Have I landed in Swotsville, dear diary?

TUESDAY JANUARY 8TH

Advantages of moving here:

1) My bedroom hasn't got that funny cheesy smell which my old one had. This is because I don't have to share with a loathsome, whiny midget called Elliot any more.
2) That's it.

9

Disadvantages of moving here:

1) I wasn't consulted. Last November my relics just announced we're moving closer to London, as Dad had been offered this new job right out of the blue. 'It's the chance of a lifetime,' he announced. 'And at my advanced age too,' he added, as a sort of joke. And that was it. He didn't even bother to ask if I'd mind moving hundreds of miles away.

2) I'd lived at my old house all my life (twelve whole years) and really didn't want to leave.

3) I hated leaving all my old mates behind.

4) Every day at my new school lasts for three centuries.

5) Laughing is against the law there.

6) I'm only at that school because Dad's new boss is very chummy with one of the governors. My parents don't know that I overheard them saying all this.

7) I feel dead lonely.

8) Too depressing to list any more.

WEDNESDAY JANUARY 9TH

The neighbours here are a right misery. After school this afternoon I was playing a game of footie by myself in the back garden, when the woman next door rang up to complain about all the noise I was making. She said I was stopping Olympia from concentrating on her work.

Olympia's five years old!

THURSDAY JANUARY 10TH

Theo's a wet weed.

He always looks as if his parents have just washed and ironed him. And I know he can't help that. But he talks all the time in this quiet, whispery voice, is dead serious about everything and has no sense of humour at all (in other words, he doesn't laugh at any of my jokes).

Some of the other pupils are OK. But everyone here seems so anxious and nervous and kind of damped down all the time. It's as if this school's sucked all the fun out of them. Well, it'd better not try to do the same to me.

I had my first homework back today in science. And straight away, Theo was buzzing in my ear, 'So what did you get then?' as if it really mattered.

I got 10/20 and it's no big deal, so I told him. And he couldn't stop himself from giving this little smile.

Later I spotted him writing down my mark at the back of his exercise book. 'What are you doing that for?' I asked.

He went very red and said, 'My mum really wanted to know.'

I think his mum needs to get out more.

Actually, I'm pretty content with 10/20. I never got massively high marks at my old school either. I'd say I'm average at most things. Maybe a bit above average in public speaking and English (though my spelling is rubbish) and a bit below it in the really evil subjects like French and maths. Up to now, my parents have been fairly happy with my school reports. Teachers usually said I was too gobby but they sort of liked me just the same.

And anyway, I'm not really bothered because school's got absolutely nothing to do with my career. You see, I'm going to be a comedian. Don't laugh. Well, you can if you like. But there's only one thing in the world I can really do well and that's make people grin.

Even when I was about two years old I was making my nan and my aunties laugh. I'd sing silly songs and then, when I was a bit older, tell silly jokes too and do impressions of people off the telly. And my nan would be wiping her eyes saying I was a 'little imp'. And my mum would be declaring she didn't know where I got it from, while I just felt so happy and proud.

At school, too, I was always the one who'd liven up the lessons by saying something daft. In fact, if a lesson was especially boring people would start looking at me to lift their spirits.

Then last year there was this talent show for children. Twenty-three contestants, and the winner was . . . ME. Got the certificate on my bedroom wall to prove it.

Actually, I was dead nervous when I first went out on that stage. My old heart was pumping away and I was sweating buckets . . . and I started burbling away in an Australian accent.

Still not sure if the audience were laughing at my jokes or my terrible accent. But anyway, they were laughing and I felt something click inside me and I wasn't scared any more. In fact, I could have stayed on that stage for much longer. Can't tell you how intoxicating it was. Best moment of my entire life.

SATURDAY JANUARY 12TH

Tonight my family was invited to walk up to the top of the road and hang out at Theo's mansion.

Theo's dad opened the door. 'Welcome aboard,' he bellowed at us. He's as bald as a snooker ball and absolutely massive. He grabbed my hand, crushed it for about two years and when I squeaked, 'Hello, Mr Guerney,' shook his head vigorously and boomed, 'We don't stand on ceremony here! I'm Mike and that's Prue.'

Prue (Theo's mum) was slinking about in these black flowery trousers and jangling like crazy because she was wearing so many bracelets. She said there was masses of food and we must all 'really tuck in', then handed us plates the size of contact lenses.

14

After the meal came an unexpected cabaret. Theo played the piano (he looked at me and blushed a bit before he started) and then Mike and Prue told us about Theo's many musical accomplishments. Then they went on to recount Theo's many other achievements. But by now I was yawning too loudly to hear properly.

Next it was Theo's sister Libby's turn to entertain. She's only six, the same age as Elliot (as Mum observed in a hushed voice to Dad afterwards), yet she could recite the names of all the kings and queens from 1066 to the present day.

At the end Mum asked, 'But how have they managed to achieve all this so young?'

'Well, they've both got brains like sponges,' cried Mike, 'and are soaking up knowledge all the time, but also . . .' He looked at Prue.

Prue beckoned to us to follow her into the kitchen. On the wall was a chart showing all Theo and Libby's out-of-school activities: music, art appreciation, chess and other equally grisly things were all up there.

'It's hard work keeping up with it all,' said Prue, 'and knowing where I need to be and with what equipment. But we're determined that our two won't squander a second of their time.'

Mum and Dad stared at the chart, goggle-eyed with amazement. Then Elliot piped up that he'd written a story today.

'Oh, do tell us about it, dear,' cooed Prue.

'It's all about this person who eats bogies,' he began.

I caught Mum's eye and saw she was trying very hard not to smile. Shortly afterwards we all tottered out of there. Never to return, I hope.

SUNDAY JANUARY 13TH

The worst thing about my dad:
He has absolutely no sense of rhythm. That wouldn't matter if he didn't insist, even at his advanced age, on dancing at parties and weddings. Worse than this, he once started playing an imaginary guitar in an HMV store. The store was playing a track from the hit parade of the seventeenth century which Dad recognized. So he started prancing about like a madman, not caring I was standing right beside him. Later he told me that when he

was a teenager he'd been in a band for a few weeks. The mind boggles ... and boggles some more.

The worst thing about my mum:
She has moments when she totally loses it. You never know when one of these outbursts will occur. The most recent was when I was just innocently watching TV, and she suddenly lurched in front of the telly, ranting, 'You're not watching this rubbish, are you? You must have something better to do with your time than that.'

She went on like this for several minutes. But I was calm and patient with her and after a bit she quietened down again, leaving me to settle down undisturbed in front of the telly once more.

Conclusion:
After an evening exposed to the barmy behaviour of Mike and Prue, I am forced to admit my parents aren't actually that bad.

I mean, Mike and Prue are in their children's faces all the time. And can you imagine spending every day with them? No, dear diary, don't even try and imagine that. You'll only give yourself nightmares.

MONDAY JANUARY 14TH

I shoot my mum the odd bar of fruit and nut chocolate (her favourite). There's a special offer on them at the moment so I bought her one today. She was dead chuffed and before I knew what was happening she was planting a big slurpy kiss on my face. Just this once I let her carry on and even gave her a little hug in return.

When Dad came home this evening he asked me if I'd learned the dates of all the kings and queens of England from 1066 yet. He said this in a completely serious voice; it was only when I saw that little twinkle in his eye that I knew he was joking.

'You scared me for a moment there,' I said. Dad burst out laughing then.

TUESDAY JANUARY 15TH

Mr Wormold made me stay behind after

registration today. He said my appearance was a 'total disgrace', and then began criticizing me in more detail, starting with the knot in my tie (too small, apparently). I thought to myself: here I am taking fashion advice from a man who wears his trousers up to his nipples. It's just lucky that I can see the funny side of things.

When he'd finished I said, 'Thanks a lot, your wizardry.'

Now, most of my old teachers would have smiled at that. But not Wormold. He just swelled up like a balloon and said, 'We've been very patient with you, but our patience is now exhausted' (and he really rolled that last word around in his mouth).

Somehow, I get the feeling he doesn't like me very much!

WEDNESDAY JANUARY 16TH

That woman next door, Mrs Reece, has been round to complain about me again. This time it's because when I was in the garden I cleared my throat too loudly or something daft like that. I tell you, where we live now is just crammed with moaners

– and most of the moans seem to be about me.

But Mum tried to be nice to her and made her a cup of tea. Mrs Reece sat in the kitchen sighing about how her life is so busy these days, chauffeuring Olympia back and forth to music lessons and the art club and swimming. 'Still, however much you do you always feel you could do more, don't you?' she said. Then she went into her sighing routine again.

I escaped upstairs and worked on my impressions of Wormold – you might call this my little act of revenge. It's taken me a while to get his voice but now I've got it all right. If I say so myself, it's a perfect impression.

THURSDAY JANUARY 17TH

Finished decorating my room tonight. Every wall is now sprinkled with pictures of genius comedy characters like Ali G, Basil Fawlty and my all-time favourite, Fletcher from *Porridge*. These personal touches make a bedroom a home, don't they? Now, the moment I come through the door I'm in my own private world of humour.

Bit of a disaster in assembly today.

The headmaster was giving us this long lecture about the amount of noise we make in the corridors when we're changing lessons! He wittered on and on about decibel levels until finally I whispered to Theo, 'My foot's gone to sleep and I'd like to catch it up.'

To my complete amazement Theo let out a laugh. Only it was more like a yelp really. Theo looked pretty astonished too and turned bright red.

At last, I'd made Theo laugh. I'd have been pretty happy if the headmaster hadn't suddenly stopped his nattering and started eyeballing me. Then he pointed a long, wrinkly finger at me and I realized he thought I was the person who'd let out that strange cry. Well, I couldn't exactly tell him the truth, could I? So I was sent out to wait outside his chamber of horrors.

After assembly he gave me this long lecture about what a bad start I'd made and how this was a school with the highest standards. While he was talking he put his ugly mug right up to mine and gave me a thorough watering. And his breath was just awful. In a second, I thought, I'm going to have to ask him to move away before he starts melting my face. He really shouldn't be a headmaster with breath like that. I'm sure it's against the health and safety rules.

As I was finally staggering out he croaked, 'I shall be keeping my eye on you.' Just so long as he doesn't breathe on me again I really don't care.

SATURDAY JANUARY 19TH
6.30 p.m.

The undead walk . . . into our house. Or they're just about to. Mike and Prue (plus Libby and Theo) are due any minute now. Mum said she had no choice as it would look very rude if we didn't invite them back.

She and Dad have spent practically all day preparing for this visit. Mum's just changed into this new, spangly, blue top which Dad bought her. I said, 'Hey, Mum, you're looking sleek.'

I can be dead charming when I want to be.

Now the doorbell's rung. The gruesome twosome have arrived. Full report later.

10.15 p.m.
Do you know what Mike and Prue spent the first half hour doing – prowling round our house. Can you believe that? Then Prue asked if she could 'take a peep upstairs' and Mike lumbered up after her.

After which they very kindly brought us up to speed with Theo and Libby's latest accomplishments, such as Theo getting three A minuses in one week. After telling us this Mike punched the air and shouted, 'Yes!'

'We're very proud of those A minuses,' he went on, 'but we don't want Theo to stop there. We're demanding nothing less than straight As from him, aren't we?' Prue jangled in agreement.

'Never be satisfied,' cried Mike. 'Keep pushing yourself all the time.' Then he went on, 'I've never passed an exam in my life.'

I tried my best to look surprised.

'And do you know why?' He paused, and I longed to call out: 'Because you're thick.'

'Because I had no one to push and

encourage me,' he said, at last.

'But you've done very well,' put in my mum encouragingly.

He gave her a regal bow. 'But if I'd had someone behind me I could have done something really important. That's why, since the day our children were born we've pushed and stimulated them and always put their happiness ahead of our own.' He turned to Libby and Theo. 'Haven't we?'

'Yes,' they chorused, just as if they'd rehearsed this moment (perhaps they had). 'And what did you say the other day, Theo,' asked Mike, 'about your ambition?'

Theo looked away from me and mumbled something.

'Come on, say it out loud, boy, because it's worth sharing with everyone,' roared Mike.

'I want to be a company director before I'm twenty,' said Theo, still avoiding my eye.

'What about that?' cried Mike, bursting his buttons with pride now. Then he turned to me, 'Now Louis, tell us about your ambitions?'

I considered the question. 'I've got this one really big ambition. By the time I'm twenty I'd like to be a lettuce washer in a hotel.'

Mike looked at me in utter consternation for a moment. Then Theo let out another of his yelping laughs and Mike chuckled uneasily.

But afterwards Mum asked me a tad crossly, 'Why did you say you wanted to be a lettuce washer?'

Talk about daft questions. 'Because it got a laugh, Mum. Why else?' I said.

Mum Behaving Oddly

MONDAY JANUARY 21ST

I've got a stalker.

Yesterday he hid under my bed and jumped out at me. Today he's been ferreting about, mixing up all my CDs, and stealing my batteries. Elliot just doesn't realize that my bedroom is PRIVATE. And he is only permitted to step inside it when he's invited (which will never happen).

Had a very strong urge to jump on Elliot tonight, but knew if I did that he'd only go squealing to my parents and I'd be in the wrong again.

So instead, I recited all his latest misdeeds to Mum, fully expecting her to defend him ('Be patient with him, love, he's only six' is what she normally says). But amazingly, tonight she didn't. She just said quietly, 'I know he needs a little guidance. Leave it to me, will you?'

Have I made Mum see Elliot's truly horrible nature at last?

TUESDAY JANUARY 22ND

I can't believe it. I was hoping Mum might give Elliot a bit of a pasting or lock him in the loft for a week, but she's gone much further than that.

There's a new after-school club starting up on Thursday called French Club, and she's making Elliot go with Libby and Olympia. Of all the instruments of torture mankind has devised, French Club is undoubtedly one of the very worst.

It's bad enough having French lessons during the day. But to have this ghastly subject inflicted on you in your own free time is gross beyond belief.

What's more, I really seem to have turned Mum against Elliot, because later I heard her saying to Dad, 'He's only on Book Five, you know, while Libby, who's six months younger, is on Book Nine already. And his handwriting is atrocious . . . well, just compare his writing with Olympia's, who's a year younger.'

On and on she spouted. And after a bit Dad was starting to agree with her. Do you know, I actually felt a tiny bit sorry for Elliot (a very weird sensation). What exactly have I started?

WEDNESDAY JANUARY 23RD

Theo made a right show of himself today. We were waiting for the results of a maths test and he was just dripping with sweat.

I said, 'Theo, it's only a scabby little test. What does it really matter? It's not as if they're paying us.'

But then he told me that actually his parents *are* paying him. Every time he gets an A– he gets what he calls a 'twenty-pound bonus' (with a forty-pound bonus if he ever gets an A).

Well, he earned another twenty smackers today.

THURSDAY JANUARY 24TH

Elliot stumbled in from French Club looking dazed and bewildered. He also went to bed very early. I said to Mum that I thought he'd suffered enough now for all his misdeeds but she didn't seem to be really listening.

SUNDAY JANUARY 27TH

Sunday night. A grey feeling comes over me as another week of school looms.

Tonight I tried to explain to my parents just how much I hate it there. But they just said things like, 'Come on, love, give it a chance. It's new, so it feels a bit strange, that's all.' And, 'It's got a wonderful reputation and you'll soon settle down. The syllabus is practically the same as your old school, you know.'

Well, the syllabus might be. But nothing else is. Can't tell you how much I hate walking in there. Especially on a Monday. To cheer myself up I whistle 'Jingle Bells' or something equally daft to myself.

Then I stroll into my form-room and old Wormold is usually there already. He just has to see me now for his lip to start curling up like a stale sarnie. Why couldn't I have someone a bit more cheerful for my teacher? Like, say, Jack the Ripper.

If I let it, that place could really get me down. That's why, dear diary, I'm going to write about something much more important: I've started collecting jokes for my comedy act. My aim is to get at least a hundred. Here's a quick example:

I lost my dog so I put an advert in the paper. It said, 'Here, boy.'

I like that one a lot.

MONDAY JANUARY 28TH

Made Theo laugh again today. Gave him an exclusive preview of my Mr Wormold impression and he fell about. That was definitely the highlight of my day. I just love making people laugh. Every time it happens I get this warm glow inside.

Feel bad now about what I told you about Theo, before. You know, when I said he was a wet weed. Please try to wipe that from your memory bank – because he's not. He might have a brain the size of a planet and wear shirts that gleam like a lighthouse but actually, he's all right. You can talk to him about normal things like football and he's mad keen to hear about all the new telly programmes even though he probably won't be allowed to see any of them. His mum does let him watch wildlife programmes (they're educational). But practically nothing else.

'She keeps on about how she wants me to be a doer, not a watcher,' he said.

'Oh, being a watcher is much more fun,' I said.

TUESDAY JANUARY 29TH

Libby and Prue came round to show us Libby's new tennis racket. Libby's only been playing tennis for six weeks and already she's been evaluated as having real natural talent and . . . but I couldn't bear to hear any more of that. So I escaped into the sitting room to watch some telly.

Suddenly I spied Prue gawping at me. And she had this really shocked look on her face as if she'd caught me doing something extremely naughty.

'Mellow greetings,' I called.

She didn't answer, but I heard her whisper to Mum, 'Now, I never allow mine to watch television at this time of the day.' I waited for Mum to say, 'Well, we do things differently here – so just keep your nose out.' But instead she sped in and switched the telly off.

'We don't have that on now, do we?' she said, smiling anxiously at me.

Well, we do actually. But I didn't want to embarrass Mum in front of Prue. So I never said a word, just whizzed upstairs and carried on watching the telly in my bedroom.

After Prue had gone Mum was a bit crisp with Elliot and me. Then she went kind of quiet and gloomy. Not even my impression of Mr Wormold could restore her spirits (and usually my impressions can). Mum obviously finds Prue's visits very stressful. Next time she calls I think we should all just pretend to be out.

WEDNESDAY JANUARY 30TH

Something odd happened today.

I was in my bedroom working on my joke collection when Mum opened the door and knocked (she always does it that way) and asked, 'Louis, would you like to go to French Club tomorrow with Elliot?'

Well, I started chuckling away, 'Mum, you naughty, little sausage, that's a good one . . .' but then my blood turned to ice. You see, Mum wasn't smiling back.

Instead, she started babbling inanely, 'Elliot is going, you see, and it's for all ages, so I thought it might be fun for you too.'

'Mum, I'd rather eat worms.'

'Would you?' She seemed really taken aback.

I said, 'You know French is my worst subject. There are amoeba with better French accents than me and . . .'

Mum put her hand up. 'I just thought . . .' she began, with a wistful look on her face. But then she recovered herself. 'No, you really wouldn't like that, would you?' she said and then slid away again.

I'm still recovering from the shock of that encounter. How could Mum have thought I'd enjoy going to French Club?

THURSDAY JANUARY 31ST

Mum hasn't mentioned French Club to me again. I expect she just went temporarily off her trolley yesterday.

But she still made Elliot go. And she's much more short-tempered with him these days. I really think she's gone off him a bit. I almost wish I hadn't complained about him now. I've opened up a real can of worms there.

FRIDAY FEBRUARY 1ST

Two more test results (you have tests here just about every second) and such excitement: Theo came top in both, even gaining an A in one of them. His first ever. So by my reckoning, that's sixty quid he's made today.

I notice Theo's stopped asking me what marks I get.

At home tonight, Dad was on the phone to a mate from his old job. And Dad was telling him about all the extra responsibilities he's got. He sounded dead gloomy about it too. I don't think Dad likes it here any more than I do.

SUNDAY FEBRUARY 3RD

Heard Mum and Dad whispering away tonight. Unfortunately I couldn't catch who they were talking about. And they stopped talking as soon as I appeared. But I definitely saw shifty glances passing between them.

Actually, I'm pretty sure I know what's going on. Dad's had enough of his job and is about to pack it in. But he and Mum are worried about telling me, thinking I'll be upset about moving back to a smaller house and all that stuff. When in fact I'd be *really, really, happy* to leave here and I wouldn't care if we ended up living in a mud hut.

But I won't let on to my relics that I know anything, as this is all a bit embarrassing for Dad. No, I'll wait and let him tell me when he's good and ready (but let it be soon as I can't wait to go home).

MONDAY FEBRUARY 4TH

Mum and Dad looked ghastly tonight. So I've been really nice to them. I patted Dad on the shoulder and asked about his day. Then I smiled at Mum several times, asked about her day too and made them both a cup of tea.

Went to bed totally shattered. Being nice to your parents for a long period of time (like a whole evening) really takes it out of you.

TUESDAY 5TH FEBRUARY

Mum had to suddenly pop out tonight and as Dad wasn't back Prue dropped in to keep an eye on Elliot and me (even though I told Mum there was no need). I'm dead certain Prue knows Dad's about to resign, as every time she looked at me she dripped sympathy all over the carpet. She doesn't realize that when we shake the dust of this place off our shoes I'll cheer for an hour.

Later, I went up to my bedroom and watched a repeat of Alan Partridge on the telly. It was just brilliant. Perhaps I could make up an annoying character for my comedy act. And who better to inspire me than Mike and Prue.

I have now collected forty-seven jokes.

Tonight I caught my mum doing something she's never done before.

I found her in the kitchen, crouched down on her knees, *looking through my school bag*. At first I tried to excuse her behaviour. I told myself, She's just on a quest for mouldy sandwiches (which lurk at the bottom of my bag for centuries). But then I saw that in her hand was one of my exercise books, which she was studying intently. Gave me a very nasty turn. But, dear diary, it gets even worse.

For then, in this strange, muffled voice, which I hardly recognized as belonging to my mum, she started making comments about my spelling and punctuation and handwriting.

I walked over to her. 'All right, Mum, just put the exercise book down now,' I said, trying to keep my voice as low and reassuring as possible. 'That's for my teachers to sort out, not you.' But it was like talking to someone in a trance. Do you know, I don't think she even heard me. Instead, she sat down at the table in the kitchen and started writing all the correct spellings in pencil in the margins. Very distressing to watch, I can tell you.

And then she began asking inane questions like, if I got 9/20 for a test what was the top mark? And whereabouts do I come in the class? And all the time she was looking at me really keenly.

But I was patient and understanding, as she's obviously not at all well. And I fear she's not just temporarily deranged this time. No, the stress of Dad resigning from his job has completely turned her head. Actually, I wouldn't be a bit surprised if it's also brought on a midlife crisis. I've heard they're very popular with women of my mum's age.

So when Dad gets back from his sales conference on Friday I'll tell him that I know all about him quitting his job. Then I'll tactfully inform him that Mum's begun acting like a loon. But he's not to worry, for as soon as we go back home (our real home), everything will be all right again and Mum's midlife crisis will be over.

THURSDAY 7TH FEBRUARY

She's been in my bag again.

I'd only just got through the door tonight

when she started burrowing around inside it. She had more daft questions for me about my position in the class. But I kept my voice low and soothing. I also bought her a bar of fruit and nut. Usually she puts it in the fridge and rations herself to four squares a night. Today she just gobbled it down in one go. A very bad sign, I think.

Also wondered if instead of having a midlife crisis she might be going through the change. I don't know much about this except women usually catch it when they turn forty (which Mum just has) and their hormones go a bit mad for a while. So I might come downstairs one morning and discover Mum has sprouted a big black moustache, like that woman in the cake shop where we used to live.

I can't say I'd be too happy about that. And I really think it would be better if Mum stayed indoors while the moustache is in full bloom, as people are always making snide comments about that woman in the cake shop (to be honest, I made one or two myself).

Terrible, terrible news.

My dad isn't resigning from his job and Mum isn't having a midlife crisis or any of that carry-on. Something much, much worse than that has happened.

You remember on Tuesday night my mum slipped out (and the ghastly Prue substituted for her). Well, I now discover that Mum had been summoned to my school for an *urgent meeting* with the King of Spit, my headmaster. My dad went there straight from work and then they both had to listen to Spitty moan on and on about my 'poor level of commitment' amongst a thousand other things.

Dad then had to rush off to his sales conference. But he and Mum decided that when he got back they'd talk things over with me together. Meanwhile, of course, Mum has been nosing in my bag and generally making a total nuisance of herself.

Anyway, tonight, after Elliot had gone to bed I was summoned to the sitting room. Straight away I knew a big lecture was brewing up. You can just tell, can't you? I often get one after a parents' evening. I always listen politely, because I think it's important to allow parents to have their say and let off a bit of steam. By the next day it's all forgotten.

But tonight was totally different. For a start, they said I wasn't to worry about what Spitty had said, as it wasn't my fault. No, they were to blame. They even went on to say how they were very, very sorry.

'That's all right,' I joked. 'Just make sure you try harder in future.'

But why were my parents apologizing to me? That's something parents hardly ever do. It was then I had my first glimmer of danger, like a little rattle in my skull. Dad said, in this very grim, serious tone, 'Don't worry, Louis, we're determined to raise our game from now on.'

What on earth was he talking about? I told myself this was another of his jokes. When I looked into his eyes I'd see a little twinkle in them. But tonight, those eyes were horrifyingly blank!

'And we promise we won't let you down in the future,' said Mum solemnly. 'From now on you'll have exactly the same chances as the other children here.'

After which, they both started grinning

at me in a distinctly spooky way.

Dear diary, something very freaky is going on in this house.

The Nightmare Begins

MONDAY FEBRUARY 11TH

My telly's gone.

Went up to my bedroom after school and there, on the desk, was a TV-shaped space, like a freshly dug grave. That TV's been with me since I was knee-high to a grasshopper.

I knew at once who the culprit was. Mum tried to laugh it off at first, acting as if she'd done something totally unimportant. But my persistent questioning quickly broke her down. She claimed she did it because she didn't want me falling asleep every night in front of dross. After which, she spouted this wild theory that without my telly I'd have more time to read, think and be creative.

I very patiently explained to her that TV gave me ideas for my work and that anyway, I needed to watch all the comedy on it to help me my the career as a comedian (for which I've now collected sixty-five jokes). But Mum just shook her head as if what I said was of no significance.

Still, I had one trump card left: Dad. Now he just loves the telly. And whenever Mum's out he lets us have the telly on all the time. We can even watch the cartoons when Dad's in charge.

So after tea I settled beside him and said, 'Guess what, Dad. Mum's kidnapped my telly and she won't even send me a photo so that I know it's all right and not chained to a radiator somewhere.' Dad chuckled before releasing his bombshell: he was in total agreement with Mum on this matter.

So now, every time I want to see anything on telly I've got to make the big old journey downstairs. I can never experience again the joy of watching a TV programme in the comfort and privacy of my own bedroom. It's just not right, is it?

How dare Mum and Dad sneak into my bedroom and get rid of my telly without even consulting me? Surely parents aren't allowed to do that. For a start, it's a total violation of my human rights.

I tell you, I very nearly called ChildLine. I still might.

TUESDAY FEBRUARY 12TH

Rescue mission commenced at 4.05 p.m.

Mum was round at Prue's with Elliot, so I climbed up into the loft, where I guessed (correctly) Mum had hidden my telly. It was stuck in the back, all by itself, looking dead lonely. I carried it down and back to where it belonged.

Mum did a double-take when she spotted it in my bedroom later that evening. 'How . . .?' she spluttered, and pointed.

'It escaped,' I said. 'It didn't like being kidnapped. It's got very sensitive sockets, you know.'

Mum let out this deep sigh and sat down on my bed. 'We're doing this to help you, love,' she said. 'We just want you to reach your full potential, that's all.'

'But what's my telly got to do with anything?'

45

Mum couldn't really answer me, so she just pretended to be concentrating on taking my TV out. But I know why. She and Dad think if they just get rid of my TV I'll suddenly be good at school. Have you ever heard anything so daft?

WEDNESDAY FEBRUARY 13TH

Mum is still nosing in my bag. In fact, I'd say she's becoming a bit of an addict. I'm hardly through the door before she's poring over my exercise books. And then she'll mutter piteously, 'Oh, you've got another C.'

'At least I'm consistent,' I grin back.

'I suppose Theo got another A minus.'

'I believe he did,' I say airily. And then I try and change the subject to something more important like, what's for tea?

THURSDAY FEBRUARY 14TH

Earlier this week I just happened to mention to my mum that we've got to write an essay on the social changes during the reign of Henry VIII and ever since she's gone into total overdrive about it. She spent a whole day on the Internet finding all this stuff about Henry VIII and the dissolution of the monasteries and much, much more. She's also been to the library and brought back about two thousand books for me to read. It's dead nice of her to be so interested, but it's just too much interest, if you know what I mean.

FRIDAY FEBRUARY 15TH

Who's in big trouble at school again? Who else but me?

In assembly this morning, Spitty was nattering away when someone started whispering (not me this time, honestly) and Spitty immediately stopped talking and stood very still with his arms folded. He went on doing this for about two years.

I whispered, 'I think rigor mortis has set in,' and, 'Someone press play, for goodness' sake.' Just a couple of little jokes to alleviate the deadness. But unfortunately, Spitty heard my second joke and I was called up to the front.

I was told to wait outside his crypt and left the hall to the sound of my own footsteps. Every single person turned away from me as I walked past them, just as if I had something catching. All I've done, I thought, is whisper a couple of jokes to try and cheer things up a bit. At my old school everyone whispered in assembly. Even the teachers.

Spitty kept me waiting half the morning. Not that I cared. It was only lessons I was missing. Nothing important. And when I was finally admitted he was having his elevenses. He sat there chewing a slice of cake and eyeballing me in silence. Finally he hoisted his mighty buttocks out of the chair, put his face right up to mine, let loose that killer breath and uttered something I couldn't quite catch. I nearly said, 'Spray it again.' Just stopped myself. Instead, I asked in my politest voice, 'What was that?'

He moved his face even closer to mine. And just as he started talking a bit of cake flew out of his mouth and straight into mine, landing on my tongue!

I wasn't at all sure what to do with it. I did think of somehow spitting it out . . . but in the end I swallowed it. Actually, all things considered, it didn't taste too bad. And I was feeling a bit peckish, as it happens. But the whole incident was so totally bizarre that I started laughing uncontrollably. Really couldn't help myself. On and on I went while Spitty gaped at me as if I'd gone totally mad.

Then he rumbled, 'Why do you behave like this? You're not just letting yourself down – but your parents too.'

Well, that brought an end to my giggling all right. I started to feel a bit guilty then. And I really hoped Spitty wouldn't send for my mum and dad again.

I also decided that as my mum had got so keen about my Henry VIII essay I'd pull out all the stops on it. I've got no intention of making a habit of this, though. This is a one-off, unrepeatable offer.

SATURDAY FEBRUARY 16TH

Came downstairs this morning to find Dad parading about in tragic trousers. He was going off to play golf (for the first time in his life) with, of all people, Mike. And Mum was acting all excited about it. Another small sign, I fear, of my parents' escalating madness.

TUESDAY FEBRUARY 19TH

Half-term and a week away from the hell-hole. Sheer bliss – or would be if I weren't so worried about my mum and the company's she's keeping.

A whole gang of women, including Prue and Olympia's mum from next door, sat around swilling tea in the kitchen this morning. From the bits of conversation I overheard they seemed to spend the entire morning boasting about their offspring. All except Mum, that is: she was noticeably quiet throughout.

The very worst of them was Olympia's mum. She just went on and on about Olympia's musical talent. Then she started telling everyone that when she was pregnant with Olympia she played Mozart to her bump every morning. Now, how sad is that? And why is Mum spending time with such dubious characters?

WEDNESDAY FEBRUARY 20TH

'Now, Louis, tell me what out-of-school activities you'd like to join,' cooed Mum today. She's even starting to sound like Prue now! She went on, 'You're the only one here not playing a musical instrument and that's fine – not everyone is musical. But how about Art Club or Chess Club, they sound like good fun, don't they?'

'The very idea of them makes my flesh creep.'

Mum sighed. 'We just don't want you to feel excluded.'

She looked so concerned I said, 'Actually, Mum, there is one club I'd like to join.'

'Yes,' she cried eagerly.

'One which will tell you how to be a comedian.'

'Oh, you don't need any lessons in that,' she said.

'Thanks a lot, Mum,' I grinned, as that was a really massive compliment. But Mum didn't smile back.

THURSDAY FEBRUARY 21ST

Heard Mum on the phone arranging for Elliot to go to Chess Club and Art Club next week. He doesn't know yet, poor little blighter. Who'd have thought I'd ever feel sorry for my brother. These are certainly strange times I'm living through.

SUNDAY FEBRUARY 24TH

Earth-shattering news. I worked on my history essay over half-term! It went against all my principles, but I did it. Just hope my parents appreciate the sacrifices I've made for them. I've produced five fat pages and – prepare to be very impressed now – I've even checked the spellings. *Bad spellers of the world untie.* (Joke!)

THURSDAY FEBRUARY 28TH

Got the Henry VIII essays back today. To no one's surprise, Theo got the top grade (but a mere A minus) while the lowest grade, D, went to *me*.

Wormold said that despite its length my essay was very muddled (I'd agree with him there) and looked as if it was copied. (Again I'd have to agree, as most of it was. Who am I to try and improve on what some learned geek had to say about Henry VIII?)

As soon as I got through the door Mum was looking all hopeful about my history essay. So I broke it to her gently. In other words, I lied a bit. 'Everyone did really rubbish,' I said. 'And I got a D. Sorry.' I said this last fact very quickly, with the unfortunate result that Mum thought I said I got a B. This made the true result even more of a downer.

Mum said, 'Oh – a D,' very tragically and then hissed, 'And I suppose Theo came top.'

'Yes, it's so monotonous, isn't it?'

Mum dropped onto a chair, a broken woman. I patted her on the shoulder and said, 'You've got to remember, Mum, I'm just an idiot really.'

FRIDAY MARCH 1ST

Mum's vigour restored, she came into my bedroom and declared, 'Don't worry about that history result, Louis, move on from it.'

'Cheers for that, Mum.'

'And one day,' she went on, 'I know you'll make us very proud of you.'

So they're not proud of me at the moment then. That's a bit of a downer.

MONDAY MARCH 4TH

Tonight, I was in my bedroom struggling with my maths homework when I felt heavy breathing down my neck. I looked up to see Dad leaning over me like a vampire about to attack its next victim.

He hissed, 'Just want you to know, Louis, that I shall be getting back from work at a reasonable time every night from now on. So whenever you want any help I shall be here for you.'

Tried very hard to look pleased, then waited for Dad to shuffle off again. Instead, he did something deeply annoying. He switched off the music I had playing in the background.

'I think you'll work better without this,' he said. I tried to explain to him that I must have some kind of noise in the background like music or TV. If it's totally silent my mind immediately wanders. But he only smiled at me in a patronizing way. So, I thought I'll just wait for him to shove off and bung the music back on then.

But he didn't leave. Instead, he lolled about on my bed slurping peppermints in a very annoying way. I sighed very loudly more than once but he didn't take the hint. He just went on watching me.

TUESDAY MARCH 5TH

Tonight, Dad decided to stand behind me while I did my maths homework. I'd only just started when he coughed right down my ear and said, 'Let me help you, because I can see you're struggling. Now, this is how I used to do it.'

He explained it in such detail that I was even more confused than before. And then he got stuck himself (I tried very hard not to laugh). But he wouldn't let it alone. I tell you, I haven't had a moment's peace from him tonight. Meanwhile, Mum's been downstairs supervising Elliot. I hate to see my parents behaving so oddly. Mike and Prue have seriously disturbed the balance of their minds.

WEDNESDAY MARCH 6TH

Mum's turn tonight. I'd written one line of my English homework when she cried out, 'Oh, no.' Made me jump right out of my skin. 'Sorry, I didn't mean to alarm you, love,' she said. 'But you've made a spelling mistake. Let's get the dictionary and look up the correct spelling, shall we?'

You can imagine, dear diary, how long

that English homework has taken me. And even when Mum sat down again she kept staring at me, looking both sad and hopeful at the same time. I think she's waiting for the moment when I turn into Theo.

THURSDAY MARCH 7TH

You won't believe what I'm going to tell you now, but it's completely true. After I'd finished all my homework tonight and was in urgent need of a nice, relaxing computer game, Dad waved this huge maths book at me. 'I think this will help you,' he said. 'It's the best on the market. So how about trying some of the exercises at the front to start with?'

I was too astounded to speak at first. Finally, I said, 'You do realize, Dad, that if you get me to do this extra homework you'll be breaking all the child labour laws.' He did grin a little at that and then said, 'I'll let you off with the first two pages, then.'

My bedroom is turning into a sweat shop.

FRIDAY MARCH 8TH

Had both Mum and Dad crashing in and out of my bedroom tonight. Now, I don't mind them dropping in to tell me when tea's ready. And I've never objected to Mum making my bed when I'm out. But they're roaming about in here all the time now. And my bedroom is just not open to the public.

I asked them, quite politely, if I could please have some privacy back. But my parents are more on transmit than receive these days. And Mum just said wearily, 'Oh Louis, please don't take such an unhelpful attitude. Why are you always working against us?'

SATURDAY MARCH 9TH

Aliens have abducted my real parents to do tests on them in a small village in Mars. They've left me with these ghastly look-alikes. Well, the aliens must have done all their tests by now so can they please bring back my wonderful (though I never realized this before) old parents as I'm missing them a lot.

57

Felt sort of depressed tonight. Decided to cheer myself up by watching a *Crimewatch Special*. I'd just settled down when Mum sprang in front of the screen. 'How about,' she cooed, 'if the three of us share some quality time together?'

I would much rather have watched *Crimewatch*. But my opinion was totally irrelevant as Mum had already switched the telly off. Then she and Dad sat either side of me, smiling hopefully.

'I think we should play a game,' said Mum.

'Murder in the Dark,' I suggested.

They chuckled.

'Truth or Dare?'

They chuckled again.

'Hide and Seek. You two hide and I'll try and find you . . . tomorrow.'

In the end we let our hair down with a wizard game of Monopoly — Dad's favourite when he was a lad in the nineteenth century. They both kept beaming at me and saying what fun we were all having. 'Now, isn't this better than staring at some boring old TV programme?' cried Mum.

Well, no actually. Now, I like my parents. I really do. But spending hour after hour with them like this just isn't natural. And it's so exhausting too. I went to bed totally shattered. I have now lived a whole month in a bedroom deprived of a television set.

MONDAY 11TH MARCH

You won't believe what Theo told me today.

Every morning, on the dot of seven o'clock, the four members of Theo's family sit round the kitchen table 'chanting and affirming'. One day his dad might recite the three As: 'Aspire, Achieve, Acclaim.' After which, each of the children will chant those same words about fifty times!

Another time he might shout, 'I must do better,' at Theo and Theo will shout back the words at him, only even louder. Today they started the day with the cheering thought: 'Never be satisfied – try harder.'

Well, I listened open-mouthed to all this. What a carry-on. And I started picturing the rest of Theo's day: on the chain gang until half past three, then whisked off to play the French horn or something equally gruesome. After which, home to three hours of homework.

Now, what kind of life is that? I told Theo we'd all be a lot happier if we went back to the old days when children worked up chimneys. For a start, the hours were shorter. And at least chimney sweeps got a day off occasionally.

Even at the weekends Theo's parents are organizing things for him. Just about every moment of his day is spoken for. I asked him if he ever got sick of all this. He lowered his voice and admitted it did get a bit much sometimes. 'Some nights I even have dreams about homework,' he said.

'What a waste of a dream,' I said.

'Well, I just can't get school work out of my head. Now and again I escape to the park for a little while . . . and just for a bit I'm totally on my own. But then I have to go back again.' He sighed. 'Still, if you want the good things in life you've got to work hard, haven't you?'

TUESDAY MARCH 12TH

What goes tick, tick, woof?

A dog marking homework.

Sorry, not very funny. But I've just had another terrible evening with the relics.

I'd hardly got in the door when they both moved in on me like a pair of jackals. And every time I moved tonight one of them was there tracking me. They'll be timing how long I'm in the loo next. Feel as if I'm in one of those high security detention centres where you never get left alone for a moment.

WEDNESDAY MARCH 13TH

If you went to visit someone in prison you wouldn't ask all brightly, 'So how was your day, then?' because you know the answer you'd got. 'Rubbish, like every other day.' And you certainly wouldn't go on to ask, 'How did you get on with slopping out today? Did it go well?'

But now, my parents want to know every little detail about my day at school. And I hate bringing back the bad vibes of school into my home. I used to think my day started once I'd left there. Now . . . now my school follows me home every night.

THURSDAY MARCH 14TH

Elliot had a right strop at Mum tonight. He yelled, 'Mum, I wrote five pages at school and I did some reading and now I'm very tired so just leave me alone.'

Later I told Elliot if he wanted to jump up and down on my bed he could (for some reason this gives him great pleasure). And I didn't even care if the springs broke. In this time of adversity he and I have discovered our brotherhood.

FRIDAY MARCH 15TH

Elliot has been moved up to the top table for reading and writing. My parents went on and on about it, and rang up all the neighbours.

Later, I pulled Elliot off my bed. I said if I ever caught him jumping up and down on it again he would be mincemeat for certain.

MONDAY MARCH 18TH

Came home tonight to find my mum and Olympia's mum deep in conversation in the kitchen (Olympia and Elliot were both at Art Club).

Mum was enthusing about Elliot and the marvellous progress he was making. Then Olympia's mum lowered her voice – the way you do when you're talking about someone who's just died – 'And how is Louis getting on?'

There was a bit of a silence after that question. But then Mum gulped hard and said, 'Oh, Louis . . . Louis's always been something of a late bloomer. He was late walking, late talking and at school . . . well, I know he'll surprise us all in the end.'

So that's what I am: a late bloomer. Or late developer. That's what Mum really means, isn't it? But I'll never develop into another Theo. For a start, I've got one of those brains which wears out easily and can only do school work in short bursts (twenty minutes, absolute maximum).

But I don't care. Honestly, I don't. What I do hate, though, is the way my mum and dad act as if I'm nothing at the moment. That's quite hurtful, actually.

I'm surprised they don't hide me away in a cellar like the Elephant Man – only to be let out when I get As not Cs. And another thing which really annoys me is when they . . . but I don't want to write about this any more.

Going to tell you a joke instead. You'll like this. A duck goes into a chemist's shop and asks for some lipsalve. The chemist says, 'Certainly, that will be ninety-five p.' And the duck replies, 'Will you put it on my bill, please.'

Here's another one. One of my faves. What did the wig say when it was blowing across the street?

'I'm off my head.'

I bet that made you smile. Until things improve here I'm just going to write jokes. No point in depressing you as well, dear diary.

TUESDAY MARCH 19TH

I have five noses, six ears, seven mouths. What am I?

Quite ugly.

WEDNESDAY MARCH 20TH

There are ten cats in a boat and one jumps out. How many are left?

None, they're all copycats.

THURSDAY MARCH 21ST

Keep Britain tidy – stay in bed.

FRIDAY MARCH 22ND

What's the point of parents anyway? No, this isn't the start of another joke. It's something I've been pondering a lot lately. Here's what I've decided: you need parents for food, clothes and somewhere to crash out. They also drive you places and give you pocket money. And that's it. Those are all their main functions.

I suppose they can be handy to have around for any emergencies which may occur, so it's useful to have them on stand-by. But otherwise, they should retire into the background and stay there. The very last thing you want are parents demanding your attention all the time, like mine.

Now, even when I'm relaxing after finishing acres of homework one of them (at least) will be in a chair next to me. And not sitting quietly, toasting their toes by the fire like a proper parent. No, they're talking to me. And I could even tolerate that if they weren't talking about history or algebra or world affairs. They're always trying to slip me something educational. They never let up on me.

Do you know what I'm suffering from? *Parent fatigue.* I keep telling myself it's just a phase they're going through. They've been led astray by our neighbours and got into some bad ways but if I'm patient with them they'll come through. And one day soon I'll be laughing about all this with Mum and Dad.

But what if it just goes on and on like this? What do I do then?

SATURDAY MARCH 23RD

I hit the roof today.

My parents asked me if I'd like to have a lousy, stinking tutor to coach me in lousy, stinking maths and English *over the holidays.* Is no time sacred to my parents any more? Before I could answer they started raving about this ancient woman they'd found in a home for clapped-out teachers, and told me she will be coming to the house every morning from Monday, at ten o'clock.

Well, this was absolutely and definitely

the last straw. I was just seething with fury. I snarled at my parents, 'No tutor, no way,' and stormed upstairs.

Now, I don't often get really mad so there was something of a shocked silence. Later, Mum appeared in the doorway with a hot drink. And she didn't have a strop at me. In fact, she was pretty friendly, all things considered. Then, just as she was leaving she said, 'We'll talk about the tutor tomorrow.'

SUNDAY MARCH 24TH

Neither Mum nor Dad mentioned the tutor once today. A small victory for me, I think. They did ask me if I'd go on this drama course they'd just found out about. It's for six mornings over the Easter holidays at the village hall. They said it sounded 'great fun'. I'm always instantly suspicious of anything parents say will be 'great fun'. It's usually the total opposite!

But I thought I might learn something useful there for my career as a comedian (lots of comedians are also actors, aren't they?) and it'd get Mum and Dad off my back. So I said, 'Yeah, all right. I'll try it out.'

Hope I'm not going to regret saying that.

Enter Maddy

MONDAY MARCH 25TH

Went to the first Drama Club session today. There were about fifteen of us in this big hall. The guy in charge is called Todd Wallace. He's younger than I'd expected and dead enthusiastic. Runs everywhere with his arms tightly by his sides. I keep expecting him to break into Riverdance.

He told us he's taught for a while but acting is his first love. And he's been in *The Bill*. So he's a proper actor all right. He started spouting about this amazing voyage he was taking us on. And I thought, Wicked, we're going on a trip! But then he said it was a voyage of discovery into ourselves. Talk about a let-down.

We each had to find a space and say some words over and over. My first word was 'pear'. Todd stood in front of me listening, then hissed, 'No, come on, really sound those vowels.' I smiled and tried to pretend I knew what he was talking about.

After that we had to close our eyes and hum a note. And we had to stick to our note and not hum what anyone else was humming. Then we had to find a partner to listen to our hum. I was paired with this rather shy-looking girl. I grinned at her. 'Do you want to do your hum first?'

She smiled back. And that's when I clocked her eyes, quite small, but really sparkly. 'This is daft, isn't it?' she whispered.

'Yeah. And I don't believe he was really in *The Bill*. I bet he made that bit up to impress us.'

Her eyes started shining away again and we exchanged names. She was Maddy, short for Madeleine. 'Do your friends call you Mad for short?' I asked.

'No, they just think I'm mad,' she smiled.

You could have a laugh with her. I

sort of liked her, actually.

Then we all sat around in a big circle. Maddy was called into the middle to improvise something. But she lowered her head and whispered, 'I'd rather not.' I was surprised at that.

Next I was summoned into the middle. I had to imagine a situation where a boy had come home late to be faced by his irate mum. I was pretty nervous but then I started imagining my mum and what I'd say to her. And I knew I'd try and be cheery and make a joke of it all. So the first thing I said out loud was, 'Hi, Mum, how's it grooving?' That got a laugh. So did the next thing I said and practically everything else too. I was in the middle for ages. But do you know, I could have stayed there all day. What a show-off!

TUESDAY MARCH 26TH

Drama Club started today with us all pretending to be furniture. There were lots of cabinets and desks. But I was a lampstand. Gave this big, goofy smile when I was switched on and then let myself droop right down when I was switched off. Todd

71

said he liked where my improvisation was going.

Then, at last, we did some proper acting. We read this play aloud called *Our Day Out* by Willy Russell. I was a naughty schoolboy called Reilly – so no need for much acting there. Maddy played Mrs Kay – one of the teachers. She got the voice and tone off really brilliantly, and sounded exactly like a teacher. I was very impressed.

At the end of the class she came up to me and said, 'You were wicked as Reilly today. You made me laugh and I don't laugh easily.'

'Oh, thanks. I thought you got that teacher's voice off perfectly.'

But she wouldn't have it. 'No, no.' She shook her head really vigorously. 'Can't act in front of people. Just hate it.'

Afterwards I wondered, if she hated acting in front of people so much, what was she doing here?

THURSDAY MARCH 28TH
Last drama class today before the Easter break. We're back again on Tuesday. You

won't believe what happened at the end of the lesson. Maddy came up to me and said, very quietly, 'On Tuesday, after class, would you like to have a coffee with me? There's a place just up the road we can go to, if you want.'

I was totally stunned but I said. 'Yeah, cool.'

'You see, there's something I really want to ask you . . .'

But she didn't say any more, just vanished. I wonder what she's going to ask me. Maybe, dear diary, she's going to ask me out on a date. Oh, what a laugh if she does. Ha ha ha.

And Ha ha ha again.

SATURDAY MARCH 30TH
No girl's ever asked me out before. Hard to believe, I know, but true.

MONDAY APRIL 1ST
When Maddy asks me out tomorrow I still don't know what I'll say – but I won't say no. I'm certain of that.

Arrived at Drama Club looking a little smarter than usual (I'd actually combed my hair). During the morning Maddy and I gave each other these little smiles. It was cute in a sickly kind of way. After the lesson we popped to the coffee shop. There were only two free spaces next to this pimply-faced guy wolfing down some bacon butties.

But conversation with Maddy was very easy. We just ran through the basic things. She's my age, twelve, although she looks older because she's so tall – half a head taller than me. She's got two 'revolting' twin sisters and goes to an all-girls school about a mile from my dump.

Then the bacon-butty-eater left and we relaxed a bit more. Maddy said, 'There's something I want to ask you.' Here it comes, I thought. I took a suave slurp of my coffee and hoped there wasn't any froth left around my mouth.

'I should tell you first,' she said, 'that I've wanted to be a famous actress for as long as I can remember. It's always been my dream. And then a couple of years ago I got my big chance to play Nancy in

Oliver! A fabulous part. I learned all my lines but then, just before I was due to go on stage, I threw up everywhere.'

She gave this little laugh. 'I waited until you'd finished eating before I told you that.' But then she looked dead sad as she told me how her nerves stopped her going on as Nancy. In the end her understudy played the part.

I felt really sorry for her but I also couldn't help wondering what her throwing up before she went on stage had to do with asking me out. 'I knew,' she continued, 'my nerves would stop me from going very far as an actress. So now I'm a talent scout, instead.'

'Since when?' I asked.

'Since a week ago, last Monday. I thought I'd go along to this drama group and see if I could spot anyone with star quality there. And straight away, I noticed your comic flair.'

It was around this point that I realized she wasn't going to ask me out. It was only my comic flair she was interested in. And I was sort of disappointed. (How pathetic. I know.)

She went on, 'If you become my first

client I will do everything I can to help you fulfil your destiny.'

I became a bit suspicious. 'Do I have to pay anything?'

'Oh no,' she replied. 'I'm your agent as well, so I only make money when you do. Then I will take ten per cent of your earnings to cover my costs, and to help other stars I discover in the future. I'm a non-profit-making agency. So, what do you say?'

For once I really was stuck for words. She was obviously off her onion. But still, what did I have to lose? So we exchanged phone numbers. Hers was on a card which said underneath her name, 'Talent Scout and Agent'. As we were leaving she said, 'I'll work hard for you, Louis.'

THURSDAY APRIL 4TH

Todd stopped me at the end of the class today to thank me for my 'ace contributions'. He also asked if I had any acting ambitions. So I told him about wanting to be a comedian and about me winning that talent competition. He was dead interested too. I could tell.

We then had this quite lengthy natter about comedy. He said the best comedy is not just about telling jokes – it's a way of looking at life. He suggested I read some good humorous novels. He's going to lend me one tomorrow.

FRIDAY APRIL 5TH

Put on a little performance for the parents today. We did some improvisations (including one where we all had to be flowers and trees – felt a right nerd) and an extract from *Our Day Out*. I was Reilly again but Maddy refused to play Mrs Kay in public. The girl who took her place wasn't half as good as Maddy would have been.

My mum was there. Todd told her I showed great promise and had definite comic energy. But Mum just made a joke of it all and said, 'Oh, I know all about Louis's comic energy.'

Todd lent me a really old book called *Joy in the Morning* by P. G. Wodehouse. It's very long but I'll give it a bash. Todd gave me his address but said there was no hurry to post it back.

Said goodbye to Maddy. I'll sort of miss

her even if she is as mad as a brush. She said she had big plans for me and she'd be in contact soon. Still think she fancies me a bit.

My Big Chance

MONDAY APRIL 8TH

Woke up feeling as fresh as a newly laid egg, then remembered I was back at the hell-hole today. Well, my whole body just seized up and I couldn't move. When Mum came in to see why I wasn't dressed I told her not to be upset but I was temporarily paralysed. She just sighed, 'Oh Louis, I really haven't got time for this. Get up now.' Somehow I managed to crawl out of my bed of pain.

But not one second of school today was worth getting up for. In fact, I was so bored I nearly started eating my hands. I really wished I was back at Drama Club, pretending to be a digestive biscuit.

Then I came home and spent another jolly evening under house arrest. What am I going to do about my parents? They're getting worse and worse. If only they could take up a new hobby which would get them out of the house and off my back. How about hiking? A boy at my old school had parents who were hikers. And sometimes they were gone for over a week! Oh, wouldn't that just be fantastic. Really must talk my parents into trying that.

TUESDAY APRIL 9TH

I really pushed the idea of hiking tonight but my relics weren't buying. Said they weren't fans of the outdoors, being 'townies' at heart. Then Mum started wittering on about blisters. I offered to buy her the blister cream they advertise on the telly but even that wouldn't change her mind. I'm considering barn dancing or aerobics for them now.

Been thinking about Maddy a bit today. I almost gave her a bell, just to be friendly.

Elliot's got this annoying new habit: he keeps getting gold stars at school.

Got another C today. Mum went all silent and tight-lipped when she saw it. Later Dad burst into my bedroom while I was resting my hands for a minute. 'Oh Louis,' he sighed, 'when are you going to put some energy into your work? You're just not trying, are you?'

Actually, I am trying. But I'm not the brightest lamp in the shop. I know and accept that. Why can't my parents do the same?

11.30 p.m.
Woke up to hear my parents whispering away. I bet they're discussing me. The black sheep of the town. I used to entertain them, make them laugh. But not any more. Now I'm just a *big problem*.

Parents have this special ability to make you feel like a total worm. It's one of their most annoying characteristics.

THURSDAY APRIL 11TH
Joint appearance by my parents in my bedroom tonight. Dad announced, 'If you get a B grade or higher for any of your

next pieces of homework we'll give you twenty pounds—'

'And a cuddly toy,' I interrupted.

But neither Dad nor Mum smiled. Then Mum went on, 'The twenty pounds isn't a bribe. It's just a little extra encouragement.' And of course I really believe that. They must be getting very desperate now.

FRIDAY APRIL 12TH

Today I made Theo an offer he couldn't refuse. He'll get ten pounds if he lets me copy some of his maths homework (not all of it. I'm not greedy. Just enough to get a B).

Theo was pretty shocked at first. I said, 'If you say yes, you'll be making four people very happy: my mum, my dad, me – and your good self.' The whole deal was finalized before school started.

MONDAY APRIL 15TH

Mrs Archer, my maths teacher, told me I got a B for maths homework today. She seemed a little suspicious. But my parents were ecstatic. Mum looked at the B as if she'd just witnessed a miracle. Dad blew his nose vigorously and croaked, 'Well done, Louis. We knew you could do it.' Later I heard Dad saying to Mum in the kitchen, 'Louis just needed an incentive, that's all.'

I've started that comedy book Todd lent me: *Joy in the Morning*. It's about a really geeky guy and his clever butler, Jeeves. It hasn't got any actual jokes in it, but it's pretty funny just the same.

I nearly called Maddy again. I thought she might have rung me by now. What's happened to all those big plans she had for me?

TUESDAY APRIL 16TH

In the school library today I came across an advert for salsa dancing: 'It's fun, it's different, it's for all ages. Come to our special introductory course on Tuesday nights.'

I'm not exactly sure what salsa dancing is, but my dad thinks he's a good mover (ha ha) and from the pictures on the sheet it looks extremely vigorous, so ideal to tire my parents out. I made a copy of it, and then asked them this evening, 'Do you like to have fun and keep fit?' Neither of them answered me, they just looked a bit startled. I pressed on. 'Well, I thought you might be interested in this sheet about salsa dancing, as a lot of parents at my school are going to it. The younger ones are, anyway.'

'Oh, that lets us off then,' said Dad at once. He's always making comments about his age. But he was looking at the sheet with considerable interest. And Mum was watching him and smiling.

'I've heard about this,' said Dad. 'Someone at work does it. Enjoys it too.' He handed the sheet to Mum. She smiled as she read it. I really think they might be hooked.

WEDNESDAY APRIL 17TH

After school today there was a football match, my school versus another snobby one. The whole place was just crawling with parents.

I was a reserve so Mum was there (with Elliot) while Theo's a star striker (yes, maddeningly, he's a top footballer too), so of course Mike and Prue were much in evidence. Mike even went onto the pitch to give Theo some last-minute advice ('Just focus, focus'), much to the irritation of the ref, our sports teacher (Mighty Midget – a little man who bristles with self-importance and can throw a strop with the best of them).

Anyhow, the match began. Rows of parents armed with camcorders yelled at their children to 'Play harder' and 'Tackle the man, not the ball.' Actually, some of the tackles looked more like assassination attempts to me.

But it was nil–nil until the second half, when Theo suddenly whacked the ball into the corner of the net. Frenzied cheering from half of the parents until Mighty Midget ruled it off-side. I glanced at Mike. He was swaying about like a stunned bull. Then suddenly he charged onto the pitch.

He looked pretty fearsome but there was fire breathing out of Mighty Midget's eyes too. The two locked horns doing all this hissy whispering, until Mike yelled, 'Ref, you're rubbish.' The ref gave this yip of fury and I think in a few more seconds there would have been one almighty bloodbath. But very unfortunately, Spitty ruined all the fun by creaking, 'Stop this at once!'

One glance at Spitty's eyebrow was enough to quell even Mike. Spitty went on to say that the referee's decision is always final and no interference from anyone else would be tolerated. Then he ordered Mike off the school site. Mike thumped away, telling Prue (who was fluttering beside him in headscarf and sunglasses) that he couldn't stand by and see his boy cheated of his moment of glory – and that this wasn't the end of the matter.

After that, the rest of the match was a big anticlimax. Mike was waiting outside the school gates, slouched against his car like a sulky teenager. A few parents went over to him to offer their support. 'It's not over yet,' he kept saying. 'I've got witnesses.'

Mum seemed quite shocked at Mike's antics while I nearly passed out from laughing so much.

THURSDAY APRIL 18TH
Met Theo before school for another

business transaction. Decided I'd be tact-
ful and not mention his dad nearly
attacking the ref, but Theo couldn't stop
talking about what had happened. 'My dad
was only standing up for me,' he said
proudly. 'He'd do anything for me.
Anything.'

In the evening Mike padded round to
chat to my parents. He said that he'd been
summoned to the school this afternoon
and they'd told him if he took the matter
any further Theo would be dropped from
the team.

'If that isn't a case of out-and-out
blackmail, I don't know what is,' he cried.
'And then,' he added indignantly, 'they
had the nerve to accuse me of poor
gamesmanship. *Me*, who's helped raise
thousands of pounds for that school's new
gymnasium.'

The school also made him write a letter
of apology to Mighty Midget. 'Hard to do,'
said Mike, 'when really I just wanted to
knock him into the middle of next week.
Well, what father wouldn't?'

As he said this he screwed up his face
and bunched his hands into fists. It was
dead fascinating to watch, although I

noticed Dad gazing at him with some alarm.

Anyway, in the middle of all this the phone went. Mum answered and it was Maddy! Heard Mum telling Dad and Mike, 'A girl's just rung up for Louis.' She couldn't have sounded more amazed if a Martian had called to converse with me.

I was chuffed Maddy had contacted me but felt a bit shy. 'Hi, how are you doing?' I asked.

'I'm fine. Yeah, fine, thanks.' She sounded shy too. 'I've got an audition for you on television.'

'Wow.' I was dead impressed.

'It's a new talent show for children. I've got all the details and the entry form. Maybe we could meet up soon.'

'Definitely. How about your house tomorrow?'

She lowered her voice. 'Well, the thing is, my house is going to be a bit crowded tomorrow. My sisters have got some friends round and they'll just take over the whole place – as usual.'

'Come round to mine then. You can have your tea here as well, if you like.'

She did like – and we arranged it all.

Later I told my parents that Maddy would be coming for tea tomorrow. Of course they assumed she was a sort of girlfriend (I didn't explain about her being my agent as they'd never understand that) and they were at my throat with a hundred questions. It made a nice change from them asking me about school work, I suppose. But they never stopped making stupid suggestions. Even when I thought I was safe in bed Mum popped her head round the door. 'Have you remembered to brush your teeth? Girls don't like it if your breath smells, you know.'

'Goodnight, Mum,' I muttered, through clenched teeth.

FRIDAY APRIL 19TH

Got another B today for maths. A lump formed in Dad's throat, and for one grisly moment I actually thought he was going to start blubbing. 'I'm proud of you, son,' he whispered. 'I knew once you found your feet . . . Well done, Louis.' Then he handed over another twenty pounds (which of course I'll split with Theo).

Mum thought it would be nice if I wore

'my best suit for Maddy'. The one that only gets dug out for weddings and funerals or when I'm visiting ninety-year-old great-aunts on Bank Holiday Monday. The one I look a total geek in. So, of course, perfect to wear when Maddy calls.

I selected some casual (but smart) clothes, messed about with my hair, explained to my mum why I couldn't be wearing a tie and sprayed a few gallons of Dad's smellies under my armpits.

As soon as they saw me both my parents held their noses and started laughing for some obscure reason. Then Mum kept on looking out of the window. I hadn't been nervous until she started doing that.

Maddy arrived on the dot of six o'clock, holding a large cake. 'Mum said I had to bring one of her cakes,' she explained. 'It's probably disgusting and I nearly threw it in the hedge.' We didn't get a chance to say any more as my mum insisted on giving Maddy a little tour of the house. Don't ask me why. It wasn't as if Maddy was thinking of buying it.

Then Dad joined in the fun by asking Maddy the same questions Mum had asked her ten minutes before. While Elliot kept running into our legs and giggling, before running off again.

Maddy and I did get to eat on our own in the dining room. But even then Mum kept bringing in things and lingering. I longed to call out, 'You've brought the refreshments, now clear off.'

But at last there were a few parentless moments. Maddy waved this newspaper at me called the *Stage*, which I'd never heard of but which she reads every week. On the back page was this large advert.

TOMORROW'S STARS

HAVE YOU GOT A CHILD BURSTING WITH TALENT?

CAN YOUR CHILD SING, DANCE, ACT, TELL JOKES, JUGGLE?

IS HE OR SHE AGED BETWEEN TEN AND FOURTEEN?

THEN HERE'S YOUR CHILD'S CHANCE TO APPEAR ON A MAJOR NEW SATELLITE SHOW. EACH CHILD WILL HAVE FORTY-FIVE SECONDS TO DEMONSTRATE HIS OR HER TALENT AT OPEN AUDITIONS TO BE HELD ON MONDAY 29th APRIL AT THE ROBSON THEATRE AT 10 A.M.

So here it was, my big chance. I've always wanted to be on TV – and now it really might happen. Of course forty-five seconds wasn't very long. I'd have to prepare my act very carefully. But I could do that all right and Maddy said she'd help me.

Can't tell you how excited we both were. Then Maddy dealt with the practical things like where was the Robson Theatre? Well, she'd already found it on the map. It was in Covent Garden in London. She also pointed out the message in small print at the bottom of the advert. 'All children must be accompanied by an adult.' So my mum will have to toddle along too. But I'm sure she'll support me in something as life-changing as this. Just have to pick the right moment to ask her.

SATURDAY APRIL 20TH

Big surprise this morning. My relics gave me a mobile phone. I've wanted one for centuries, but they've always turned me down, claiming it was 'just an extravagant fashion accessory'. But now, suddenly, they've got me one. They said it was an extra reward for all my hard work at school.

While they were in such a good mood I also told them about the TV audition. Aren't parents weird? They get all excited about a maths grade but something like this – my chance of fame and fortune – they're decidedly iffy about.

'We're not sure if it's the right time for you,' frowned Mum. 'You're just getting a grip on your studies and this could un- settle you again.'

'Oh no it won't,' I said. 'If I do well there it will give me extra confidence – and make me a megastar, as well.'

They did both smile at that and Dad said jokingly, 'But could you cope with being mobbed in Tesco?'

'Oh, I get mobbed in there now,' I grinned.

I'm pretty certain Mum will take me. I've just got to make sure I stay in my parents' good books for the next week. So I'm being toe-curlingly nice and helpful. Also asked them again about salsa dancing. Mum said she thinks they will look in on Tuesday night.

Yes!

SUNDAY APRIL 21ST

Maddy phoned to ask if I'd told my parents about the audition, and were they excited. To which I answered, 'Yes,' and 'Not exactly.' But on the latter point I said we had to make allowances as my parents were getting on a bit and their arteries were probably hardening at this very moment.

I'm doing my very best to keep on the right side of them. In fact, I've been smiling at them so much my face aches. I've definitely strained my smiling muscles.

A strange, but true fact. In spite of my undoubted good looks and vast charm, I've never been invited round to a girl's house – until now. Maddy has invited me round for tea next Friday. So, what do you think of that, dear diary?

MONDAY APRIL 22ND

Disaster struck this morning at twenty-five minutes past nine, exactly. That was when I heard about the surprise maths test. The surprise will be how few marks I get.

The whole of my year did this test in the hall to get us used to working in exam conditions. There were rows and rows of identical desks in there. Now I know how a battery hen feels. After about half an hour of this torture I decided the safest plan would be to get out fast. So I let out a couple of pain-racked moans. But the maths teacher, Mrs Archer, just glared at me.

A few moments later I gave this really piteous cry and whimpered, 'Has it suddenly gone very dark in here?'

Unfortunately, a few of the boys, including Theo, started giggling. That's the trouble when you're known as a comedian, people laugh at you even when you're playing a deeply tragic scene, as I was then. But anyway, my cries finally stirred Mrs Archer. 'What's the matter?' she snapped.

I fluttered my eyes a bit and cried, 'I've got a splitting headache.'

'Have you really?'

'Yes, I'm afraid I have.'

At this point Theo started tittering again. And Mrs Archer snarled that if I disrupted the exam any more I'd be sent straight to Spitty (only she didn't call him Spitty, of course).

I was outraged by her deeply uncaring attitude. It would have served her right if I'd dropped dead on the spot. Then she'd have been in big trouble. But I really didn't want another encounter with Spitty, so I just moaned softly for the rest of the exam.

When I left I stayed in character (as Todd had taught me) and staggered towards the door. But Mrs Archer just shook her head and sighed, 'Oh Louis, you're your own worst enemy, you know.'

I really hate her. And she's got a face like a halibut. But anyway, it'll take her a few days to mark all those papers. And maths tests are of minor importance when you're about to be discovered.

TUESDAY APRIL 23RD

I still can't believe what happened today. After another very long day at school I left to find it was bucketing down with rain. Then this car beeped at me, and there was my old mum.

I thought, She's dropped Elliot off at French Club and now she's meeting me to stop me getting wet. What a really kind gesture. But as soon as I got in the car there was a definite atmosphere. Mum asked me how my day was but I sensed she wasn't really listening to the answer.

Once we got out of the school car park she said, 'I've just been talking to your maths teacher, Mrs Archer.'

That gave me a shock all right. 'I was summoned to the school to talk about your maths test,' she continued.

I tried to give a nonchalant shrug, which is not easy when you're wearing a seat belt.

'You only got thirty-two per cent.'

Well, I was furious. How dare Mrs Archer have marked my paper already. I bet she marked it first, too. Talk about picking on people.

'Your teacher doesn't understand,' said Mum, 'how you've been getting such high marks for homework and yet did so badly in this test. She wondered if someone was helping you.'

I shook my head.

'She thinks Theo has been doing your homework for you.'

All at once I was in a very tight corner. What should I do? For a moment I just sat there listening to the windscreen wipers smacking about. Then I decided the best way was to spare my parents all the gory details and deny everything. So I did. And I acted very outraged. Again, Todd's drama lessons helped me, as I really focused on the emotion I wanted to portray.

I also told Mum how ill I'd felt in the exam room. She figured I'd had an attack of nerves and by the time we arrived home she was practically apologizing to me.

Afterwards, I sat in my room, shaking with relief. I'd dodged that bullet all right. And I was still on the best of terms with my parents. Just had to keep it that way until next Monday's audition.

But later this evening the phone rang. Mum was ages talking to someone. And her voice just went lower and lower. Dad, who'd been on patrol in my bedroom, slipped downstairs and didn't come back up again either. Something was afoot.

Then Dad called out, 'Would you come downstairs please, Louis.' He and Mum were waiting for me in the dining room. They were both sat at the table. I faced them.

Dad told me Prue had rung up earlier tonight. Apparently, old halibut features had also rung Prue with her suspicions about Theo doing my maths homework. Prue and Mike questioned Theo and he only went and opened his big yap, didn't he! Told them everything. Even about me giving him the money.

I was totally gobsmacked. And my heart sank down into my stomach.

'Is this true, Louis?' asked Mum, in a really quavery voice. What Prue had told my parents had gone through them like a dentist's drill. I could see how badly shaken up they were.

So was I, actually. I just whispered, 'Yeah, it's all true, I'm afraid.'

I waited for Mum to have a go at me for telling her porkies in the car. But she didn't. She just said how disappointed she was in me, with Dad echoing her. And they both looked totally gutted. It was terrible, the whole thing.

Of course, Mum and Dad never went salsa dancing either. And that had been looking so hopeful. What a total and complete mess. Really depressing myself now. Definitely time for a joke.

First candle: 'What shall we do tonight, then?'

Second candle: 'Well, I was thinking of going out.'

WEDNESDAY APRIL 24TH

First thing this morning I waited outside the school gates for the parents' nark. As soon as Theo saw me he shook his head and cried, 'I'm so very sorry.' He claimed he had to tell as they kept on and on at him. 'And I don't have any secrets from my parents.'

'How disgusting,' I snapped.

'I just find it really hard to lie to them when they've been so good to me,' he confessed. 'They also said I've got to give you back all the money . . . well, here it is.'

I took the thirty pounds. I hadn't spent the other thirty pounds either, so I could return it all to my parents. And I did, tonight. Big gesture.

I said to the relics, 'I don't deserve this,' then looked upwards for my halo, which was surely circling around me at this moment. My parents were dead impressed too.

And as the atmosphere was nowhere near as arctic as I'd feared I said, very lightly, 'Been looking at the map, Mum, checking to see exactly where the Robson Theatre is, as we don't want to be late on Monday, do we?'

Mum blinked at me in total astonishment for a moment. Then she said quietly, 'We couldn't even consider taking you out of school now.'

'But it's only for one day,' I argued.

'No, it's out of the question.'

I turned to Dad but he was nodding in agreement with her. 'That audition,' I cried, 'could be my breakthrough, my big chance.'

'Showbusiness is lonely and tough,' pronounced Dad, as if he were some kind of expert. (He'd been in a band for about a month, that's all.) 'You could face four hundred rejections before you get anywhere.'

'Look, if I don't get anywhere on

Monday, that'll be the end of it. But you've got to let me try this one time. Please, please,' I cried, my voice wobbling out of control.

They did hesitate for a couple of seconds before Mum said, 'I'm sorry, Louis, but we really can't allow you to waste your time on that. Especially now, when you need to concentrate all your efforts on your school work.'

Then Dad chipped in, 'I know it's the boring thing parents say. But you'll thank us for doing this one day.'

'I won't, you know,' I replied.

Then I went upstairs and straight away rang Maddy on my mobile. She was totally crushed. 'I can't believe it,' she kept saying. Then she said, 'I'm sure they'll change their minds when they've calmed down.' But I really doubt that.

So that's it. My big chance of stardom dashed. Now I'll just spend the next few years slogging away like mad for exams I won't pass so I can get a rubbish job, work half a century at that rubbish job, rest for a couple of years and then snuff it. And that's it. My life.

Just what's the point of it? Too

depressed to even tell you a joke tonight. Sorry.

THURSDAY APRIL 25TH

The most exciting event of today was when I dug two holes in my desk with my compass. That's the only way I'll leave my mark on this school.

In geography I wrote a letter to Todd. Told him I was returning *Joy in the Morning* and I'd really liked it. I also mentioned the audition and how my parents have sabotaged my whole career.

This evening Maddy rang to see how I was and to check I was still coming round to her house tomorrow. I told her I doubted if I'd be my usual brilliant company. But she said not to worry, she'd be brilliant enough for both of us. I'm kind of looking forward to seeing her tomorrow. She intrigues me. And it'll be great to be out of this cauldron of delight for a few hours.

12.15 a.m.
I'm back, because I've reached a momentous decision. Here it is. I'm going to the TV audition after all. I've been lying in bed

planning it all out. I'll leave the house as usual on Monday, but instead of walking to school, I'll whizz to the railway station (it's only a bit further than the hell-hole). Then I will dive into the station loo, change out of my school uniform and into my audition clothes (which I will have tucked at the bottom of my school bag). Next, I shall hop on a train to London, get the tube to Covent Garden, locate the Robson Theatre and ... do the audition, make the judges laugh hysterically and dance with joy.

There are just three obstacles to this plan:

1) I've got no money for a train ticket. At the moment I've exactly three pounds and eight pence.
   Solution: Borrow some from Maddy.

2) The school will notice I'm not there.
   Solution: Forge a note from my parents.

3) I'm supposed to go to the audition with a parent and I'm lacking one of those.
   Solution: See if I can pal up with a parent in the queue, maybe get them to adopt me! Or see if I can think of a reason to explain my parent's absence.

But never mind the obstacles. I'm going to that audition. And I wanted you, dear diary, to be the first to know.

How to Train Your Parents

This afternoon I got ready to go round to Maddy's house. Mum said she thought I should wear a tie. I explained that I was going out to tea – not a job interview.

I was just walking up Maddy's drive when the front door opened and two very attractive blonde-haired damsels tumbled out. One of them called out to me, 'Are you Maddy's mystery boy?'

'Could be,' I grinned.

'Talks about you all the time, you know,' she went on. Then they kind of hovered around me. (They even smelt nice.) We did the exchanging of names bit. These were Maddy's twin sisters, Vicky and Zoe.

As I was staring at them (did I mention they were very attractive?) I said, 'You both look kind of familiar,' because they did.

'Not trying to chat us up, are you, Louis?' teased Zoe, obviously the cheeky, lively one.

I hoped I wasn't blushing. 'Oh no, but I'm sure I know you from somewhere.'

At this point there came a loud cough from the doorway and for the first time I spotted Maddy hanging about there. I waved to her, then turned back to the twins. 'Come on, we mustn't hold up young love,' grinned Zoe. And right then I knew where I'd seen them before.

I called after them, 'Chewing gum.'

'And the same to you,' laughed Zoe.

'No, that's where I've seen you: you've both been on TV advertising chewing gum.'

They just giggled, linked arms and swayed off down the road together. But Maddy said solemnly, 'Yes, that's right, they've been in an advert on the telly.'

'But that's brilliant,' I exclaimed. 'I must have seen that advert so many times. So they're actresses then?'

'No, not really actresses,' said Maddy. 'They've just done modelling and that advert – and a few other things.'

'How old are they?' I asked.

'Fifteen.'

'But they look years older.'

'And they've both got boyfriends,' said Maddy. That was a little dig at me. But I knew those girls were way out of my league. I was a bit irritated with Maddy for being so snidey. I didn't think she was like that. She was a bit cross with me too. In fact the atmosphere was distinctly chilly until I mentioned my plan to sneak away to the audition.

'Your scheme shows real dedication,' she said. 'You deserve to become really famous.' We chatted about the obstacles to my plan. As soon as I mentioned money Maddy was reaching into her purse. I told her to jot down exactly what I owed her but I don't think she did.

And then there was the absence note for school. Maddy suggested doing it on her computer. So we piled upstairs then made a list of possible reasons for me being away.

1) Something wrong with my teeth. ('Too vague,' said Maddy.)

2) Got a weak heart so I need to take to my bed from time to time.
3) Left the oven on and the house has burnt down. (Me being silly.)
4) Having a new brain fitted. (Me being silly again.)
5) Been sick in the night.

In the end we opted for number five. Maddy said you can't go wrong with that one. Here's the letter we composed:

> Dear Mr Wormold,
> I regret to inform you that my son, Louis, has been sick in the night, several times. We're keeping him at home for further observation.
> Thanking you in advance for your time and consideration.

(All Maddy's work, that last sentence. Isn't it great?)

Then I did a good copy of Mum's loopy signature and the letter was all ready for posting tomorrow – until Maddy said, 'Won't it look a bit odd posting a letter on Saturday saying you've been ill on Sunday?'

'Not if we add, "PS I'm a part-time psychic",' I quipped.

But Maddy had a point there. She said she'd deliver the letter herself on Monday. Her school was only about a ten-minute walk from mine. She'd just leave home a bit earlier. So that was all settled.

Meanwhile, you might be wondering where Maddy's parents were all this time. Well, this was the truly incredible thing. Her mum – who was just like an older version of Zoe and Vicky – said, 'Hello, Louis, make yourself at home,' to me when I arrived. *And that was all.*

I wasn't forced to endure a tour round the house. Neither did she ask me lots of silly questions. And when she brought the food in she smiled and was friendly. But she didn't hang about, except once, and then Maddy just had to say, 'Thanks, Mum,' in a slow, firm voice, and she was off, gone.

As for her dad, well he gave me a hail and a wave and that was it. We never really spoke at all. Marvellous! Somehow, Maddy's parents just seemed to know that they weren't part of my visit.

'I'm dead impressed by your parents,' I said to Maddy. 'They're so much better behaved than mine.' Then I asked her what they were like about homework.

'They leave it entirely up to me,' said Maddy. 'They never check up on me either. In fact, provided I stay out of trouble they don't bother me at all.'

'This is like being in paradise,' I cried. 'You're so lucky.'

And that's when Maddy said, dead quietly, 'Oh, but they had to be trained.'

'Trained?' At first I thought I'd misheard her.

But then she went on, 'Once my parents were exactly like yours.'

'I can't believe that.'

'All parents wake up one day and realize they're old and past it,' she went on.

'Mine have been past it for years,' I said.

'But it's only recently they've realized it,' said Maddy. 'And that's their dangerous time. That's when they say to themselves, I might be all ancient and crumbly but my children aren't. So they can make my dreams come true for me. They can do all the things I didn't.'

'And your parents did that?' I asked.

Maddy's voice became really bitter. 'Oh, they never gave me a minute's peace.'

'With school work?' I asked.

She shook her head. 'Actually, I'm all right at that. But they wanted me to have singing lessons and dancing lessons and be in adverts, like my sisters. They were always on at me about going to auditions, saying they were just pushing me to give me a chance.'

'Sounds familiar,' I murmured.

'Oh, it was just awful. But worst of all was the way they looked at me, all hurt and disappointed—'

'I know, exactly,' I interrupted.

'It's just not fair, is it?' she cried indignantly. 'Let them make their own dreams come true. That's not our job, is it?'

'No it isn't,' I agreed firmly.

'But the thing to remember is, if you take the right action, this is just a phase they go through – and afterwards they'll leave you completely alone.'

'So come on, tell me,' I cried excitedly. 'What is the right action?'

Maddy hesitated. 'I was going to keep this secret for a book I'm going to write to raise money for my agency. But as you're my client, I'll tell you the four basic rules of parent-training.'

And she did. The only problem was, she said it quite quickly and I'm not good at taking notes. But these are the main bits.

Rule one: Act all the time as if your parents aren't there

This means never ever looking at your parents unless you really have to. Every hour of the day and night you must give them the silent treatment. When one of your parents says, 'Don't ignore me,' you're on the road to victory.

Maddy's tip:

This takes quite a bit of practice. So don't worry if it takes you a while to get the hang of it.

Rule two: Never tell your parents anything

Avoid talking to them whenever possible. When forced to converse keep sentences dead short (three words maximum).

Maddy's tip:

It helps if you imagine you're a spy and your parents are enemy agents trying to make you give away vital information.

Rule three: Never argue with your parents
Remember, parents feed off arguments. And they always win them, too. So never let them provoke a reaction from you. (They will try. Be warned.)
Maddy's tip:
When your parents are having a go at you keep your face completely blank: just blink and stare at them. And don't respond to anything they say.

Rule four: Unsettle your parents whenever you can
This is best done by:

Continual sighing.

Regular door-slamming (but always accidentally!).

Looking at your parents with extreme pity and a permanently raised eyebrow.

Muttering things under your breath.

Saying things which irritate every parent such as: 'Don't bother, OK?', 'I don't care,' and 'Whatever.'

Every so often, throw in what Maddy calls a 'killer sentence'. For general discomfort Maddy recommends, 'I didn't ask to be born into this family, you know,' and 'I wish I was in a children's home and not with you.'

Also, if your parents ever threaten to punish you, just say very sadly, 'I'm sorry you feel you have to resort to that.' Maddy says, this gets them every time.

Feel as if I've discovered truly important advice tonight. Maddy really is a top agent. I shall start training my parents tomorrow – well, today, actually. It's now 12.45 a.m.!

SATURDAY APRIL 27TH
Been secretly working on my comedy act for the audition all day.

I'll definitely start my parent-training programme tomorrow.

SUNDAY APRIL 28TH
Rang Maddy tonight and did my act to her over the phone. She told me to cut one joke (What makes more noise than one cat up a tree? Two cats up a tree) as she said it was unworthy of me. I have followed her advice.

She also asked about the parent-training and was pretty surprised when I said I hadn't started yet. Then, as if reading my mind, she said, 'Do you think my parent-training is a bit nasty?'

'Just a tad,' I admitted.

'But, Louis, we're only setting a few boundaries. And all parents need those. They'll really be much happier back in their own world. And just think of all the extra leisure time they'll be able to enjoy.'

I said I hadn't thought of it like that and I would definitely start the training soon – but first I had a date with destiny.

My Date with Destiny

5.45 a.m. My bedroom
When a comedian doesn't get any laughs
the technical term is 'dying on your backside'. Wouldn't it be ghastly if I did just
that today? Can't get that thought out of
my brain.

9.10 a.m. Railway station
Arrived at the station about ten minutes
ago. I've already changed out of my school
uniform and into my performing clothes.
Now I feel like me! I also bought a ticket
without any questions being asked about
me travelling alone to London. I put that
down to my mature air and the fact that

117

there was a massive queue behind me.

Maddy rang me a couple of minutes ago. She has been to the hell-hole and delivered my absence note. She also assured me that I will not die on my backside today. 'Don't forget, you're a certificated comedian,' she said. Actually, I had forgotten that and was grateful to her for reminding me. I've promised to try and ring her at one o'clock today with any news.

11 25 a.m. Robson Theatre (outside)
One thing I forgot today – an umbrella. As soon as I reached Covent Garden it started pouring down. I also took a wrong turning (despite Maddy's brilliant map) but I still arrived at the Robson Theatre half an hour early. And I couldn't believe the sight which greeted me. A massive queue of children and parents stretching for miles and miles.

Right at the front was this boy wrapped up in so many layers of clothes he looked as if he was off to the North Pole. A pair of eyes peeped out at me.

'Is everyone here waiting for *Tomorrow's Stars*?' I asked him. He whispered something really faintly. 'Sorry?' I asked.

'Actually,' cut in his mum, 'do you mind if Sidney doesn't talk right now. He really needs to save his voice. But yes, everyone is here for *Tomorrow's Stars*.'

Took me about two years to reach the back of the queue. In front of me stood this girl in a black cloak, red baggy trousers and black pointed shoes. She also had a black hat on her head. Two adults stood next to her and all three were nestling under a large umbrella (it was still pelting it down).

The girl suddenly turned round and looked at me. 'Oh dear, you are getting wet.'

'Nothing misses you, does it,' I grinned.

The girl flashed her pearly whites at me then stretched out a hand. 'I'm Serena the Sorcerer.'

'Louis the Laugh. How are you doing?'

We shook hands, then she said, 'You can stand under our umbrella if you like.' So I did. I was introduced to her mum and her grandad, who was dressed all in black, from which this silver head protruded like a spotlight ('My inspiration,' Serena said). Serena told me that she'd been performing magic tricks at festivals since she was four years old. 'I've had this itch inside me to be famous for as long as I can remember. I want it so much that sometimes I can feel it just bursting out of me.'

'Like in the film *Alien*,' I suggested.

Her grandad asked me where my parents were. 'Oh, my mum's on her way,' I said vaguely. He didn't look very convinced.

1.10 p.m. Robson Theatre (outside)
I've just called Maddy. She was stunned when I told her I'm still waiting outside. She also wished me all the luck in the world.

2.00 p.m. Robson Theatre (outside)
Shortly after I'd rung Maddy we finally started moving forward. Serena the Sorcerer hissed at me, 'Your mum isn't coming, is she?'

I decided to take a chance and tell her the truth. 'No, my parents don't know I'm here. I've skived off school today.'

Serena let out an excited squeal. 'I knew you had.'

'To get in,' I went on, 'I'll need a parent. Can I borrow one of yours?'

Serena laughed delightedly. 'Oh, isn't this fun. I think you'd better have Grandad. Yes, he'll be best. Get him to tell you about the time he played the London Palladium. He loves telling new people about that.'

So Serena walked ahead with her mum while I hung around with Serena's grandad, who burbled away about that time in 1967 he'd played the Palladium and got a standing ovation. He seemed to remember every detail too. In a minute, I thought, he's going to tell me what colour underpants he was wearing that night. But it was kind of fascinating, actually.

Once we got inside the reception area my heart started beating really loudly. But Serena's grandad and I were so deep in conversation it really did look as if we were together. Not that the boy at the door took much notice. He just counted in the next thirty of us in a bored sort of way. I was number twenty-nine. This girl, who looked younger than Maddy, slapped a sticker with '29' on it onto my still soaking wet shirt.

We were told there were three stages being used for auditions. I was in the group herded towards the Ashcroft Room.

We seemed to go down about seventeen staircases to get there. But what did I care? I was in.

We had to sit in numerical order in the first three rows. The parents sat behind us. On the stage was a large table with a blue tablecloth on. Sitting behind it were two men from the land of the very grumpy. One looked incredibly fierce, like a bulldog with a perm. The other was bearded and sweaty, and peered at us gloomily with little beady eyes. In the middle of the glums sat this woman, beaming away like a searchlight at us.

She introduced herself as Josie and then told us the two men were from the satellite company. They even had depressing names. The one with the perm was Malcolm and the bearded one was Derek. Josie said how good it was to see us all. She was sorry we'd had to wait so long but they'd never expected such a fantastic response.

Then she explained that we would each be called up to the stage in number order. We had forty-five seconds to entertain – in any way we wanted. Then, after every one of us had performed, the judges would confer and let us know which of us would be invited back for the next round.

Now we're about to start. Be back soon.

2.50 p.m. Robson Theatre
We've reached number twenty-five so it's nearly time. I hate all this waiting. Makes me nervous.

We haven't had one comedian yet. It's been mainly singers. The first girl bounced onto the stage, stared at us in great alarm and then promptly fled. 'She wasn't quite ready,' explained her mum, pushing the girl back onto the stage. The girl was given a second chance and this time gave a remarkable impression of a cat being sick.

'She's so not coming back,' whispered Serena to me.

But a lot of the other singers were really professional. There were a few dancers too, including one tap-dancer. She was dazzlingly good even if she did remind me a bit of a wind-up toy.

3.00 p.m.
Serena's turn. Only she nearly didn't go on. Would you believe, she got an attack of

nerves. 'I've got all these bubbles in my stomach,' she hissed as me.

I gave her hand a little pat. 'Easy, tiger,' I said. 'Now go out there and give it some welly.' That made her smile and then off she had to pop. She's on stage now, going down well, too – and I'm next.

I'm next!

And yes, I've got the collywobbles. Definition of a collywobble – a three-legged sheep dog. Get it? No, it's not very good but it's the best I can do right now. Must stop. I'm on . . .

4.50 p.m. Train home
Nearly two hours ago now I clambered up onto that stage. My knees buckled a bit and I was all shaky.

But then I told myself, If the audience smell fear on me, I'm finished. A comedian has to have a lot of front. So I planted a smile on my face and did this bouncy strut towards the audience. And then I was off.

Told my first joke in an Australian accent, didn't I? Got a laugh anyway. But of course I had to stay in that accent. Still, my second joke got a great roar and some people even clapped. I called out, 'Don't clap, we haven't got time.' A few – including a woman who laughed like a neighing horse – even guffawed at that.

After that I was on a roll and just bursting with energy. I rattled off joke after joke and I never even heard the whistle blow to say my time was up. They had to blow it a second time before I realized.

I floated back to my seat and Serena whispered, 'You went down a storm.' But had the judges liked me? I'd noticed Josie exercising her facial muscles. Not a flicker from Derek the beard. But I think I spotted a smile from Malcolm the perm. Although it might have just been wind. Hard to tell, really.

There was one more girl after me (playing a mouth organ) and then the judges went into a huddle. Serena whispered to me, 'I want this more than anything else in the world, don't you?' I just grinned at her. But actually, I did.

Then Josie got up and waffled on about how we'd worked really hard and she wanted to congratulate us all. But we must also remember it's a very overcrowded market, blah, blah, blah. Then, just when I'd stopped listening she started calling out some numbers. Those people had to come up onto the stage.

She called out eight, fifteen, twenty-eight (that was Serena) and twenty-nine!

So there were just four of us on the stage. Josie said to us, 'Congratulations, you are all through to the next round.' We all jumped about a bit – but not too much because there were all those disappointed children and their parents gawping at us. They were asked to hand in their numbers at reception and to leave as quickly as possible. 'Hope you've enjoyed yourselves,' Josie called after them.

One man shouted back, 'My girl's got sunshine in her voice. This is all a fix.' His daughter led him quietly away.

I still couldn't believe that I was one of the lucky few to get that golden tap on the shoulder. And how I wished my mum and dad could have been there, whooping it up with me. Mum could even have given me one of her slurpy kisses and I wouldn't have minded. Ah well, she's missed her chance now.

'This is only the first stage,' said Serena to me. 'So we mustn't get too happy.'

'Oh, go on, be happy,' I said.

Serena laughed. 'All right, just for you I will.'

Josie told us we would get a phone call soon telling us when the next auditions were. At that audition we would have a whole five minutes to perform, so I shall need lots more jokes. She also told us to be certain to fill in the forms at reception.

I grabbed one of them and slunk away to fill it in, unobserved. Two sides of questions about my age, height, weight (had to guess that), then stuff like had I ever been on the telly before (I wrote, 'Not yet') and finally, a contact number. I gave them my mobile number.

The end of the form had to be signed by your parent or guardian. So I forged Mum's autograph again (becoming quite expert at that) and handed it in.

I bumped into Serena and her relics and they gave me a lift back to King's Cross, which was pretty decent of them. I sat in the front next to Serena's grandad. He winked at me and said, 'The call to perform and entertain cannot be resisted, can it?' He went on, 'But share your good news with your parents. They may surprise you with their support.' I wasn't so sure about that.

As soon as I could I rang Maddy. She went very quiet for a couple of seconds, then let out this gasp. 'Oh, Louis, all day I've been waiting and wondering . . . I'm just really, really happy for you. You know what this means, don't you? You're not an amateur any more.'

'Aren't I?'

'No, you're a semi-professional now.'

'Sounds good to me,' I said.

Any minute now the train is going to pull into my station. I shall be late home and I don't know what excuse I'll give Mum. And right now, I really don't care either.

All I can do is sit here with a great smile all over my face and think, I did it. I did it. I DID IT!

6.30 p.m. My bedroom

Just to let you know that I got into the house at twenty-five to six, a full twenty seconds before Mum got back with Elliot. She'd been to a special French Club which was due to finish at five o'clock but she'd been held up because Olympia suddenly had this tantrum. She has them quite regularly, apparently. It took both her mum and mine to calm her down. Never thought I'd be grateful to Olympia!

Anyway, Mum finally asked me about my day and I nearly burst out laughing. I really think I've got away with today. Of course, the next audition will be trickier. With fewer children involved, someone might easily notice I'm missing a parent – and totally scupper my chances. Perhaps Serena's grandad is right and I should share my good news with Mum and Dad. They're bound to be proud of me, aren't they? I might tell them after tea tomorrow.

12.15 a.m.
Just can't sleep. Too happy. This has been an unbelievably brilliant day.

The Worst Day of My Life

TUESDAY APRIL 30TH

From the best day of my life to ... well, wait until you hear what's happened today. It all started when Wormold asked me to stay behind after registration. I wasn't especially alarmed as he asks me to stay behind after registration every morning.

'I understand you were away yesterday,' he said.

'Yeah.' I patted my tummy. 'Really bad stomach-ache.' I rolled my eyes to emphasize how bad it had been. 'I'm better now, though. I expect it was just one of those twenty-four-hour things.'

'I was away yesterday too,' he said.

'Oh, you probably had the same bug as me then,' I said, eager to introduce a comradely note into the proceedings.

'I was at a conference yesterday, so I've just come across your note now.' And as he said this his thin lips all but disappeared. But he didn't utter another word, just waved me away.

All very puzzling but I didn't think about it again until later that morning when Spitty materialized in the corridor. He never makes any sound when he moves. You just suddenly spot him streaming towards you like poison gas.

'Be in my room at twelve o'clock sharp,' he rumbled, before oozing away again. Words to strike fear into your bowels.

'Sounds like he's after my blood,' I said to Theo. And we both laughed extremely uneasily.

Waiting for twelve o'clock was sheer agony. Now I know how those Christians felt when they were told they had a booking with a hungry lion in an hour. You just want to get the whole messy thing over and done with.

At twelve o'clock precisely, I was admitted into Spitty's chamber of horrors.

A third person had been invited to join in the fun: my mum. That gave me a jolt, I can tell you. But I gave her a friendly smile just the same. She shuddered in reply. Spitty did what he always does when he spots me: he went very still for a very long time. He finally came out of his coma and picked up a piece of paper. 'Mr Wormold has sent me this. He believes it is your handiwork. So do I.'

I took it from him and recognized it instantly. It was my absence note. But I pretended to be studying it carefully. Finally, I had to admit, 'Actually, I believe I did write it. Yes.'

Mum let out a low groan.

Spitty shook all his chins at me. And after a lot of blather about how I'd disgraced not just myself, but my family too, sentence was passed. I'm to be suspended until Thursday. I only just stopped myself from bursting out laughing. Why do schools think that giving you an extra day's holiday is punishment? I've never ever understood that.

Still, for my mum's sake I put on a gloomy face. To be honest, she was looking grave enough for the pair of us. The journey home was somewhat tense and at the old homestead Dad popped up. He doesn't often get really mad but today was one of those rare occasions.

'I've had to leave work early because of you and your behaviour.' His whole face had turned scarlet with fury. Even his nose shone like Rudolph's. 'We've given you every support and this is how you repay us,' he went on.

At first I thought I'd let them both have a bit of a gripe. I mean, it can't have been much fun having to go to my school and hear Spitty moaning on and on. After a bit, though, I remembered it was my parents who were in the wrong, not me. After all, if they'd gone with me to the audition as I'd asked, none of this would have happened and they'd be basking in my success now. So this was entirely their fault.

Then they started firing questions at me: where had I gone yesterday? Had I met anyone? And something in me snapped. So I didn't answer their questions, just looked coolly through them.

All at once I realized what I'd done. Quite spontaneously, I'd gone into the first rule of Maddy's parent-training: act as if they're not there. And do you know what? It worked. Well, sort of.

Dad's face and ears got even redder and he started shouting (something he hardly ever does). 'Come on, answer me! Where did you go?' That's when I remembered the second rule of Maddy's parent-training: say as little as possible.

So I just said, 'Into town.'

'You were in town all day?' asked Mum.

'Yeah.'

'And what did you do all day?' demanded Dad.

I shrugged.

'And did you see anyone?' asked Mum.

'People.' I was really getting into the rhythm of these one- and two-word answers now.

But Dad looked as if he was about to burst a blood vessel. 'You're grounded until further notice.'

'Thank you so much,' I replied.

'Just get out of our sight,' cried Dad.

Later I heard Mum and Dad talking on and on in a mumbling, shocked sort of way. And much later, Mum came tutting into my bedroom with a bowl of gruel. It clattered down on my desk and she gave me one of her reproachful looks. Then she hovered in the doorway. 'You've really let us down, you know. And we don't deserve to be treated like this, do we?'

I didn't answer, didn't even look at her.

'We've given you every encouragement and you do this.' Then her voice went a bit gentler. 'Why do you do it, Louis?' And I really wanted to tell her about me becoming a semi-professional yesterday. But they were both behaving so irrationally that I just couldn't risk it. I mean, what if they stopped me going any further?

So I just shrugged and sighed heavily. And Mum sighed heavily too. And that was just about the end of our convo. For the rest of the evening no one – not even Elliot – came near me. I was obviously in solitary confinement.

Maddy rang me on my mobile though. I told her everything. She was shocked at my parents' antics. 'That's so typical of them. They only ever see it from their point of view. They never ever think about what you want, do they?'

'And whose life is it anyway?' I said.

'Exactly,' cried Maddy. 'Your parents are

going through a very selfish phase at the moment. It can't be easy for you.'

'It isn't,' I agreed.

But Maddy was pleased I'd started the parent-training. I asked her how long the training took. She was a bit vague about this. But I really think I might be able to get my parents all trained up before the next audition. That's my goal, anyhow.

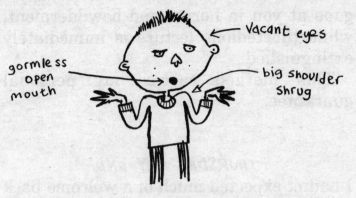

gormless open mouth

Vacant eyes

big shoulder shrug

The Parent-training Course

WEDNESDAY MAY 1ST

First full day of parent-training. Decided to make it intensive as I'm keen to get it over with.

Both my parents tried to give me a lecture today. But I've discovered a real conversation-stopper. You start by saying something out of the side of your mouth which your parents can't quite hear (although they suspect it's rude).

Then, when they ask you what you've just said, you shake your shoulders vigorously while at the same time letting your mouth drop open. Yes, you look like a total goon! But instantly your parents' voices just trail away. All they can do is gape at you in horror and bewilderment, while the tedious lecture is immediately extinguished.

This method carries my personal guarantee.

THURSDAY MAY 2ND

I hadn't expected much of a welcome back from the teachers and I didn't get it either. First off, Wormold told me to wipe the smirk off my face. I explained that I couldn't as it was my normal expression. Then it was off to maths with Mrs Archer, who acted as if I'd just wet myself.

'Oh Louis, Louis, Louis, what are we going to do with you?'

'Suspend me again,' I suggested, hopefully.

In English, tragedy struck. Theo got a B. He gazed at the offending grade, shocked and horrified. 'I don't understand it,' he whispered. 'I've never had a B in my life before.'

'Neither have I,' I said.

'No, but you're . . .' he smiled in an embarrassed sort of way, 'different.'

Later he agonized over how he was

going to tell his parents. 'They'll probably put on black arm bands and play solemn music for a few hours, but otherwise, they'll be fine,' I said.

Theo shook his head gravely. 'And there's no way I can hide it from them as they go through my books every single night.'

Dad was on patrol in my room tonight. I didn't speak to him and he hardly spoke to me. His eyes just rolled wearily around my bedroom.

FRIDAY MAY 3RD

A parcel arrived for me today. It was from Todd, sending me another P. G. Wodehouse book, *Very Good, Jeeves*. He also wrote me a little note saying he was sorry I'd missed the audition but to keep my chin up as he was sure I'd make a breakthrough one day.

Longed to tell him I'd already made a breakthrough but decided it was too risky. He might just feel he has to tell my parents. Todd also told me he's doing another drama course in the summer and he'd be really pleased to see me there. Would I be interested?

Well, even though I'm going to be a TV

star any moment now, I am very interested. You see, I don't want to just have five minutes of fame then find a week later everyone has forgotten me. No, I'm in this for the long haul. And for that I'll need to learn all the stuff I can.

I put Todd's letter down for a second and the next thing I knew Mum was reading it. I was appalled by this blatant invasion of my privacy. Don't I have any human rights now?

Each night now Maddy and I take it in turns to ring each other. But don't worry, there's nothing yucky going on. We only talk about important things, like parent-training and jokes.

SATURDAY MAY 4TH

A bit of a setback with the parent-training today. I was summoned for a discussion with my parents about my attitude. They think it's got much worse over the past few days. 'You've just not been yourself,' said Mum. (She can talk!) 'You've been rude and withdrawn but we think we know why.'

For one awful moment I thought they'd

somehow discovered I was training them. But then Mum started gibbering about how she thinks I'm finding school work too much to cope with – and 'would I like a tutor?'

'About as much as I'd like leprosy,' I blurted out, forgetting, in my shock, that I must keep all sentences to my parents to two or three words. But I quickly recovered and said, 'Tutor,' sneeringly, then looked right past them.

'But you are worried about your school work?' persisted Mum.

I raised both my eyebrows. 'Whatever,' I said mockingly.

Dad came over to me and put a hand on my shoulder. 'This isn't like you, Louis. Come on, what's wrong? We're here to help, you know.'

Could feel myself starting to crack a bit. But I knew I mustn't weaken, not bang in the middle of their training programme, so I decided this was the moment to let loose one of those killer sentences Maddy had given me. So, at the top of my voice I cried, 'I didn't ask to be born into this family, you know.' And for good measure added, 'I so wish I'd been brought up in an orphanage.'

Well, Maddy didn't exaggerate the power of those words. My dad stepped back from me. My mum looked totally stunned. And I didn't even need to start talking out of the side of my mouth to end that particular conversation. It spluttered to a halt right then.

Dad just said, 'I'm very sorry you feel like that, Louis,' and walked out.

Mum went all shirty and tight-lipped. 'We've seen a very different side to you these last days. I don't know what's got into you.' Then she stalked off too.

Afterwards I wondered if I'd been a bit tough on them. But then I remembered that this parent-training was for their own good too. They're going to have so much free time in the evening of their lives.

SUNDAY MAY 5TH

Dear diary, do you ever wish that the future was over? Not all of it. Just a little part. Like all those pointless, dead days between now and my next audition. Can't wait to get back on that stage again. And after that I'll be really busy being on the telly and performing my comedy gig around the country – not to mention tripping over photographers.

Of course I'll have to do the odd bit of maths in my trailer between perform-ances. But that's all I'll have time for. Really, really hope that the TV company rings me soon. About every five minutes I get my mobile out to check it's still work-ing all right.

MONDAY MAY 6TH

I can describe the atmosphere in my house at the moment in two words: completely horrible.

My parents both look frazzled and edgy and keep staring at me in an odd way, as if I'm a stranger they've found roaming about. Mum keeps starting to say things to me, and then spluttering out in the middle of the sentence. I heard her saying to Nan on the phone, 'You wouldn't know Louis. He's impossible at the moment.'

This has certainly been the worst Bank Holiday I can ever remember.

In history today Theo got another B. 'I'm glad I'm not copying off you any more,' I joked.

'What's happening to me?' he cried.

'Into each life a few Bs must fall,' I said.

'Not mine,' he said. 'My parents were so cut-up about my last B . . .' He bit his lower lip anxiously. 'What sort of way is this to repay them for all the sacrifices they've made for me? Louis, what am I going to tell them? You've got to help me.'

Well, I did try. But I just couldn't think of a single thing.

This afternoon I walked to Maddy's school. She was waiting outside the school gates for me. I was so pleased to see her I went all shy for a few seconds. But soon we were gabbling away. I did my new act for her, and she really liked it.

She also said I shouldn't worry that I don't have a date for the next audition yet. She was certain they'd ring very soon and I just had to be sure to keep my mobile charged up at all times.

'I hate going home,' I said.

'So do I,' she replied.

'But your parents are all trained up now.'

'Yeah, but I'd still rather live on my own,' she said.

As soon as I got back Elliot announced, 'You're in big trouble,' with a big grin on his face.

'So what's new,' I murmured.

I thought I was in trouble because I was late. But no, a fresh crime has been entered on my charge sheet. Mum told me that Prue had just been round. Prue knew about Theo getting another B and she knows why. Or she thinks she does. Theo told her it was all my fault, as I keep putting him off his work!

Well, I was really shocked. Why on earth was Theo making up all that rubbish? I even forgot about the parent-training for a moment and blurted out, 'That's not true at all, Mum. Honestly, it isn't.'

'Isn't it?' she said wearily. Then she told me that Prue had already rung the school to demand that from tomorrow, Theo and I are separated in all our lessons.

I waited at the gates for Theo this morning, but he just swept past me like a full bus.

In lessons I was moved right across the room from him. He didn't look at me once. But then, in the changing room before PE, this voice hissed at me, 'Don't turn round, I just want to say I'm really sorry for what I said about you to my parents, but it was the only way I could get them off my back. I've had to promise them I won't talk to you at all today. We are still mates though, aren't we?'

'Well, I'd give you an A for cheek, anyway,' I said.

'The only one I'll get today,' he said gloomily.

At home Elliot rushed in from Art Club and Mum immediately started going on about his homework.

'Mum,' he asked suddenly, 'when exactly do I get time to play?' Mum looked distinctly unsettled by that question. I noticed she didn't answer either.

The TV company called this afternoon! I'd just gone upstairs to do my homework when the call came. It was Josie, from the audition. She chatted away for ages. She asked about my hobbies and my school. I yakked on for ages about all my mad teachers.

Then we talked about my parents and how they've changed lately. She burst out laughing at some of the things I said about them. And she was just so incredibly friendly. Any second now, I thought, she's going to ask me to go away on holiday with her.

Then she spoke about my next audition. First off, she thought I should lose the Australian accent. I said I keep trying to lose it but it's kind of addictive. She laughed at that. Next she said she didn't want to alarm me but she had a suggestion: why didn't I drop the jokes from my act and just tell some of the stories about my family and school, which I'd told her. She thought it would seem more natural – and be funnier too. She also suggested I throw in some of my impressions of Wormold and Spitty – and my parents.

Well, I was a bit stunned but I promised to give it a try.

She told me the next audition would be next week, on May 16th. The first stage will be at eleven o'clock in the morning, then if I pass that one there'll be a screen test in the afternoon. And if I do OK there, I'd be filming my slot the very next day. Wow. And double wow!

She explained there was a hole in the schedules so that's why everything was being brought forward. She also said that if I pass the Thursday auditions, they'll put me up in a hotel so I'll be bright and fresh for my TV debut the following day.

It was all dead exciting – and everything was going just brilliantly until she asked to chat to my mum. She said she needed to go over a few details with her, such as checking I'll be able to get the time off school.

'Do you think I could have a word with her now?' she asked.

'Of course,' I said. 'I'll go and get her for you.'

I paced around my bedroom a few times, thinking hard. Then I remembered something that had happened to a boy in my class yesterday.

I picked the phone up. 'Hi, it's me again. I'm sorry to tell you Mum's just gone down with a violent nosebleed.'

'Oh dear!' She sounded really concerned.

'She gets them sometimes. But I did manage to ask her if I could go to the audition and she very definitely nodded her head.'

But Josie wasn't satisfied. She said she needed to talk to my mum directly. 'I'll be at the office until half past six,' she said. 'Could your mum call me before then?'

'Well, she's pretty busy mopping up blood at the moment,' I began.

'I do need to get her confirmation before we can proceed any further,' said Josie, with a new firmness in her voice. She gave me her number and rang off.

And I decided I'd have to tell Mum what had happened. It was such an amazing thing that she was bound to be excited for me. I sprinted downstairs. She was sitting at the kitchen table with Elliot. She was going over his homework with him. He was yawning. I hovered in the doorway.

She certainly wasn't pestering me with lots of questions. The training had succeeded there. And she was ignoring me. Again, what I'd wanted. Only, not right now.

I walked over to the fridge and opened it, just for something to do, really. 'Tea is in half an hour,' said Mum, still not looking directly at me. Then she went on explaining subtraction to Elliot.

I crawled back upstairs. There is no way I could talk to Mum about anything at the moment – and certainly not something as important as this.

My first solution was to impersonate Mum on the phone. I'd whisper, saying that the nosebleed had caused me to temporarily lose my voice. But in the end, I didn't do that, as I had a much better idea.

I called Maddy and asked if she'd like to be my mum. She kind of gasped and laughed at the same time. 'Louis, what are you talking about?'

I quickly explained and ended by saying, 'You were brilliant at playing Mrs Kay in *Our Day Out*. You really were.'

'But that was just reading aloud,' she

cried. 'While this is like acting in public . . .' her voice fell away, 'and you know I can't do that.'

'Oh, OK,' I said, trying to hide my disappointment.

'So what will you do?' she whispered.

'Don't worry, my brain cells are humming already. They'll come up with an idea any second.'

She rang off. Three seconds later my mobile rang again. All I could hear was someone breathing dead quickly. 'What's the number?' asked Maddy, in this funny, tight voice.

'Hey, are you—?'

'Don't say a single word to me,' she interrupted, 'or I won't be able to do it. Just tell me the number.'

I did and the phone clicked off immediately. Waiting was total agony. Then my mobile went again and there was another burst of deep breathing before Maddy cried, 'I rang her, Louis.'

'And did she—?'

'Yes, she did. And after a bit I wasn't nervous at all. I can't believe I did it now.'

'You saved the day all right,' I said.

'And I remembered I was your agent

and asked about the money. You're getting a fee for the recording on Friday and you get an extra fee every time your spot is shown on TV.'

'So if I get picked I'll be coining it in. Well, don't worry, I shan't forget my agent.'

We chattered for ages more and when she finally rang off I said, 'See you soon, Mummy.'

'Make sure you eat all your greens, son,' she giggled.

It was only later I realized something. I still needed to produce a parent on Thursday. They had to be around to sign forms and stuff. So what am I going to do about that?

SUNDAY MAY 12TH

First off, the good news. The amount of time my parents spend talking to me is declining dramatically. More good news. They've just about stopped patrolling my bedroom when I'm doing homework. A tired-looking Dad hovered for two minutes on Friday night before pushing off again.

A definite result there. Now for the bad news. It's too quiet in my house. You can hear the silence. You can feel it right next to you. I wanted to switch my parents' volume down – not turn it off altogether.

Whenever they see me now, my parents hardly utter a word. But their faces sag and they look tense and confused. And I don't like that. So, when will things perk up again? Maddy is distinctly vague about this.

In this current climate there's absolutely no chance of them accompanying me to the audition on Thursday. So Maddy suggested hiring someone to play my mum for the day. Like an actress who's out of work, or resting, as they call it in show business. She's going to see if she can find the name of a resting actress in the *Stage*.

But the sands of time are running out.

MONDAY MAY 13TH

In maths today, Mrs Archer was handing back homework. She went up to Theo and hissed, 'I'm very disappointed in this. See me at the end of the lesson, please.' Of course, everyone was desperate to know what grade Theo had got. He put his hand over it so no one could see. But later in the lesson someone did find out, and the news raced round the classroom: 'Theo's got a C minus.'

His shoulders were shaking and I knew he was trying really hard not to cry. C minus and Theo. Never thought I'd see those two in the same sentence. Even I got a C today.

At the end of the lesson Theo just sat behind his desk looking shell-shocked. No one said a word to him (they were all whispering about him, though). So I pottered over to offer him a cheery word. Only I didn't get a chance. Instead, Mrs Archer did an impression of someone who's just had a firework stuck up their bottom. She leaped forward and let out this really high-pitched squawk, 'No, Louis.'

'I just wanted—'

'Off you go,' she practically screamed at me.

'But can't I just say—?'

'No you can't. And you'd be better off spending your time revising for the maths exam on Thursday.'

At the mention of a maths exam Theo's mouth crumbled and he lowered his head down onto the desk. Mrs Archer shooed me away and out the door as if I were a gang of angry wasps.

I was furious about the way I'd just been treated. I couldn't even give a mate a word of comfort in his hour of need. No doubt that school soon won't allow anyone to talk to me for fear I'll contaminate them with my wicked ways. They'll probably get me to walk around the school, tolling a bell and shouting, 'Unclean, unclean,' whenever anyone comes near.

This school really is a load of pigswill. But looking on the bright side, I'll miss the maths exam on Thursday. Of course, they'll make me do it when I come back. If I come back. If I haven't run away instead.

Those last words, dear diary, just crept out of my pen. I think I might have just had a hot idea. But I need to roll it around my head for a bit.

6.45 p.m.
I've rolled it. And now I have the solution to all my problems. I'm going to run away.

The last time I made a bid for freedom was six years ago. That was when I was sick of Elliot and all the fuss everyone was making of him. So I found this massive bag, filled it with all my favourite dinosaurs and walked up to the top of my road. It started raining so I stayed in a phone box for what seemed like ages (but was probably only about ten minutes) and slunk home again. Mum never even realized I'd gone.

But this time will be totally different. I've been planning it all out. Here's what I'll do: after I've recorded my TV spot on Friday I'll go back to where I used to live and crash out at a mate's, probably Harry's (he's got a shed I could maybe hide in for a few days). I'm sure he'll bring me some scraps of food. Then, once I hit the telly screens I'll get lots more offers and be off touring around the country.

Going to ring Maddy now to tell her what I've decided.

7.00 p.m.
More amazing news. I told Maddy about my momentous decision and said, 'All I need now is a parent for Thursday. Did you find any actresses?'

'No,' she said, very quietly. Then in the same quiet voice, 'So there's only one solution, isn't there? I'll have to play your mum again.'

I was stunned. 'But, Maddy, you really hate acting in public.'

'I know. But I haven't got to say much, have I?'

'Hardly anything.'

'And it's only a background part, isn't it?'

'That's right. In fact, the main thing you'll do is sign forms.'

'I think I can do that,' she replied gravely. 'But I'll need to get some clothes to disguise myself. So I'm off to the charity shop tomorrow.' Then she added, 'Don't worry Louis, I won't let you down.'

TUESDAY MAY 14TH
Running-away equipment
1) Toothbrush
2) Shirt and jeans
3) Seven pairs of underpants
4) Dad's pongy aftershave
5) Knife, fork, cup and plate
6) Tin of baked beans
7) Chocolate
8) Book: *Very Good, Jeeves*
9) Hair gel

10) One dinosaur (just for old time's sake)
11) And if space permits, socks. But I look on socks as sort of optional, really.

I've been smuggling all these things up to my bedroom and storing them in the bottom of my wardrobe. I do realize that running away is quite an extreme measure and wonder if I should give my parents one last chance. Still not sure about this.

9.00 p.m.
Just been called downstairs. Dad said he knows I'm very worried about something and he and Mum want to help. This sounded promising but then, would you believe, he started droning on about my school work! Why does everything in my life have to be about *school*? We never talk about anything else these days.

Then he announced that they've arranged for a private tutor to come here on Friday. His name is Mr Walrus (that's what I thought they said, but it can't be right and who cares anyway as I won't be here) and he will be taking me for English and maths. Dad started grinning inanely at me, as if he'd just told me he'd bought me a puppy.

'How do you feel about that?' asked Mum eagerly. And blow me down, she was smiling away at me too. They obviously thought I'd be delirious with joy at the news that I'm getting a tutor. I tell you, my parents' sanity is hanging by a thread at the moment. Anyway, I just shrugged my shoulders, looked glum and popped into the conversation another of Maddy's killer phrases: 'I'm sorry you feel you have to resort to that.'

It didn't let me down. The sickly smiles vanished instantly and my dad said, 'All right, off you go,' without even looking at me. As I was going up the stairs I heard Mum say, 'There's just no pleasing him these days.' Communications between my parents and myself have slumped to an all-time low.

Tried to cheer myself up by reading some jokes, but even that didn't work, so I called Maddy instead. She's been to the charity shop and got all togged up for Thursday (she won't tell me what she's bought, said she wants it to be a surprise). She's also raided her savings account:

taken seventy-five pounds out of it. That's to pay for the train fare to my old home and any other expenses my running away might incur.

I told her to write me out an IOU. But she said she didn't work like that and she knew I wouldn't forget her when I become a comedy star.

And I swear on my life I won't.

WEDNESDAY MAY 15TH

5.00 p.m.

On the way into school today Theo jumped out of the bushes at me. 'Louis, tell me one of your stupid jokes, will you?' he said. Well, I'm not at my fizziest this early in the morning. But I'm also a semi-professional now, so I rattled off about half a dozen jokes. And Theo was a very good audience, actually.

Then he suddenly stuck out his hand and said, 'Best of luck in everything you do, Louis.' Gave me quite a turn actually. It was as if he knew I was running away tomorrow. But how could he know? That's a secret shared only by Maddy and me.

There was no time to ask him anything else as Mrs Archer appeared on the horizon, so he moved off pretty nippily. And I didn't get a chance to converse with him again.

Rest of the day crawled past at two miles an hour. But as I walked out of the gates this afternoon I had this really strong feeling that this school will never, ever darken my life again.

9.30 p.m.
All my running-away equipment is stored away in my bedroom now. After I've written this I shall transfer them, and you, dear diary, to my school bag, whilst bunging all my school books away. Well, I shan't be needing them again, shall I?

I am leaving my parents a note just so they know I haven't been kidnapped or anything. It says:

Dear Mum and Dad,
   Hope you are keeping well. This is to let you know that I'm off to start my career now. Thanks for all the meals and for looking after me.

Good luck in the future and I will definitely see you again, one day. Until then,
keep smiling.

From your loving son,

Louis

PS I know I'm vacating my bedroom but
I'd be grateful if you still kept Elliot out
of it. Cheers.

Running Away to Fame and Fortune

THURSDAY MAY 16TH

10.15 a.m.
Left home just after eight o'clock this morning.

Dad had already gone to work and Mum was busy searching for Elliot's maths book. As she probably wouldn't see me for a long time I thought I'd better say a proper goodbye to her.

'I'm off then, Mum,' I said. 'Thanks a lot for looking after me for the past twelve years.'

She whirled round. 'Are you all right, Louis?'

'Me, yeah, I'm blooming. See you then,

Mum. Take good care of yourself, won't you?'

And after that I was out of the door. Gone – probably for years. So, a moment of incredible significance. But, to tell the truth, I didn't feel as excited as I'd expected. Instead, I just felt a bit flat and . . . well, that's all, really.

Cheered up at the railway station, though. Maddy was waiting for me holding her school bag and a carrier bag from Help the Aged. She was also, to my great surprise, still in her school uniform. She said she'd rather wait until we got into London to get changed. I think she was just incredibly nervous about the whole thing. And who could blame her?

On the train I spouted my act aloud to Maddy. It was mainly about my parents, but with a splash of Wormold and Spitty too.

'Your jokes were funny,' said Maddy, 'but this is much better. Now you've got something to say about life, haven't you?'

I nodded proudly. 'Yes I have, though don't ask me what!'

When we pulled into King's Cross I said to Maddy, 'Are you going to get changed now?'

She gulped, said, 'It's time, isn't it?' and sprinted off to the ladies.

She was gone for ages. But at last this apparition came tottering towards me in high heels. I'll never forget it. She was wearing massive blue glasses, long dangly earrings and a grey suit. But it was her huge, curly, red wig which really caught my attention. She looked as if she had a ginger tomcat perched on her head. She didn't look especially old or young, just very, very weird.

'What do you think, then?' she asked, smiling shyly at me.

'Well, they'll certainly remember you,' I replied. At that point her wig took a spot of exercise, jumping down onto her forehead.

'Actually,' I said, 'I think you should go on instead of me. You're much funnier.'

Maddy sped off to the ladies again to adjust her wig. When she returned she said, 'It should be all right now, provided I don't walk too fast or shake my head about.' She went on, 'I look a right sight, don't I?'

'No . . . well yes, you do, actually. But I bet a lot of those show business parents appear odd too. So you'll blend in just fine with them.'

I think my little speech cheered Maddy up.

12 noon
Reached the Robson Theatre dead early, so we stood outside for a bit. Then Maddy let out this strange, retching noise.

'Are you going to be—?'

'Don't even say the word,' hissed Maddy, her face red enough to fry eggs on, 'because if you say it, I'll do it.' Then she got some car keys and started rolling them about in her hand. 'They're my mother's spare keys,' she whispered. 'I thought if I held them it might help me get into the part.'

There was no queue this time and we walked straight into the reception. The bored-looking boy was there again. He gave Maddy a long, hard stare.

'Hello,' said Maddy. 'I'm Mrs . . .' And there was this awful, agonizing silence as she struggled to remember my surname. In the end, I had to prompt her. The boy gave Maddy another long stare, then gazed down at a clipboard, handed me a sticker with my name and the number twelve on it and directed us towards the waiting room.

'I'm so sorry, Louis. My mind just went blank . . .'

'No worries, Mum,' I replied. 'Just a bit of nerves, that's all. Everyone gets them.'

At that moment I spotted Josie coming out of the waiting room. I warned Maddy, who started whispering, 'Focus and concentrate,' to herself and clenched those car keys really tightly.

Josie gaped a bit when she first saw my dodgy-looking 'Mum'. But as soon as Maddy started talking Josie seemed to relax. Maddy's voice might have been a tiny bit quiet but it was twenty-four-carat adult. No doubt about it.

Josie showed us into the waiting room. Although we were twenty minutes early it was packed already. In the middle was this girl in a cowboy hat and a burgundy leather jacket, loudly declaring, 'Music is my whole life, you know.'

'Let's get right away from that,' whispered Maddy.

Then Serena the Sorcerer burst in, accompanied once again by her grandad and mum. She rushed over to me. 'Oh, it's so good to see you again,' she cried, and even gave me a little hug. I noticed Maddy bristling a bit. Then Serena started eye-balling Maddy.

'Is that your mum?' she whispered to me.

'In the flesh.'

'She doesn't look at all how I imagined her.'

'Funny, a lot of people say that,' I replied.

Next Maddy was introduced to Serena's mum and grandad. And she had the adult patter off perfectly, gushing things like, 'You must both be very proud of Serena.'

What's more, Maddy was walking about like a mum too. She didn't overdo it either, got it dead right. I was mighty proud of her, actually.

Then we were all herded into the Ashcroft Room again, Maddy sitting at the back with the grown-ups. The same three judges as before faced us. 'I see the firing squad are back,' I whispered to Serena.

She giggled. 'You take away all my nerves.'

But inside my head I was more than a little worked-up. After all, if I passed this audition and the one in the afternoon some really fantastic things could come out of it. *If, if, if.*

The acts were mainly singers and some of them had top voices. The girl in the cowboy hat had a great pair of lungs on her. And she danced really well too. Not that Serena agreed with me! 'Her moves are actually very dated and she's got an obnoxious personality.'

'Unlike us,' I replied.

She grinned – and then it was her turn. She was totally great, and did some awesome card tricks.

And the next contestant was me. Legs went a bit jelloid and I was sweating when I started, especially as it took a few seconds to crack my first laugh. But then I was off (and in my own accent too!) telling them the things I've told you, dear diary, about my parents and my school. I slipped in some impressions and a few jokes, too. Like, 'I wouldn't say Spitty was boring but he once sent a glass eye to sleep.'

But the parts everyone laughed at the most were the little stories about my parents stealing away my telly and sitting in my bedroom and watching me do my homework. And it's just fantastic up on that stage. That's the only word for it, fantastic. And when I'd finished everyone was grinning away at me and some people patted me on the back and I felt just as if I'd made all these new friends.

The panel have seen all the fifteen acts now and are deciding who goes on to the telly auditions this afternoon. Josie said, 'Tough decisions have got to be made,' which sounds a bit ominous.

As you can imagine, the tension in here is just unbearable. Some children (and a few parents) are sitting with their hands over their faces. Others are talking really loudly and laughing a lot. I've been telling Serena the Sorcerer some more funny stories about my parents but my heart is thumping away. And the waiting just goes on and on.

Hold on. Josie's up on her hind legs . . .

1.05 p.m.
Wanted you to be the first to know.

Josie only called out three names. Serena the Sorcerer, Caro, the girl in the cowboy hat, and me. We had to walk out to the front and she said, 'We'd like you three to go through the "Yes door", with your parents.'

We left the theatre to the sound of every-one clapping (which was nice of them). I felt like a king.

I'm nearly there, dear diary. Just one more stage to go.

1.50 p.m.
We're back in the waiting room again. Sandwiches and drinks are scattered about. But no one's eating much. Maddy's disappeared to the ladies as her wig's got very itchy! So I'm sitting here going over my act yet again and wondering if Mum's found my note yet.

Thinking about it now, I suppose I've been a bit hard on her – and Dad. I mean, it can't be much fun having all the neighbours saying, 'My son's got five As today and my daughter plays the tuba. Now, is your useless son doing anything yet?'

Well, Mum and Dad will have some-thing to boast about soon. And when I know the date I'm going to be on telly I'll definitely tell them. I might even go home the night it's on and watch the show with them. And afterwards they'll apologize for not giving me any support. But I won't let them apologize for too long. After an hour I'll tell them to stop.

Just want to go and do my act again. I hate all this hanging around. Maddy's been gone ages. But she's coming back now, so I'll sign off. More news updates soon.

8.15 p.m.
Haven't had a chance to write any more until now. You see, a great deal has happened over the past few hours. Still can't believe some of it.

First of all I had to wait until a quarter past three before I got my telly audition. Now, telly auditions are totally private. It's just you, your parents and the three wise monkeys. Serena the Sorcerer went in just before me. She was in there for ages too and then she shot out. I went up to her and she couldn't speak at first, she was so out of breath.

'They didn't make you run round the room, did they?' I asked.

She laughed, then gasped, 'I got through.' She hugged me twice and her mum and grandad were skipping about like six-year-olds. I was dead happy for her.

Serena wished me luck but didn't think

I would need it as I was so good. Then it was my turn.

Josie told Maddy where to sit, then instructed me to stand on this star which was taped to the floor. There were cameras alongside me. But Josie told me to ignore them and just peer into the one bang in front of me. She said she knew it was more difficult doing my act without a large audience but she was sure I'd do just fine. Then she asked me how I felt.

I don't know why, but I suddenly felt really scared and unconfident. Maybe it was the sight of the living dead on either side of her. But I didn't tell her that or she'd think I was a total amateur. So I kept up my confident front and I was away.

Once I started the nerves fell away again. I didn't enjoy doing it as much as I had in the theatre, but it was still a real buzz. Maddy laughed away as if she hadn't heard it all about fourteen times already. Josie laughed too but Beardo just sat massaging his chin and Permo looked as if he'd gone into a trance.

And then it was all over. I went and sat beside Maddy while they conferred. 'You were just brilliant,' she said.

'Say it a bit louder,' I grinned.

About forty hours passed while the judges mumbled together, then Josie asked me to step forward.

'Hats off to you, Louis, for getting this far. You've done really well and we've greatly enjoyed your entertaining performance. However, tough decisions have had to be made and we're not going to ask you to go forward to the recording tomorrow. I'm very sorry.'

I couldn't take in what she was saying at first. Her words seemed to be coming down a long tunnel. And then I heard myself saying, 'Oh well, such is life.'

'You're not too disappointed, are you?' asked Josie.

'Oh no. You've got to roll with the punches, haven't you?' Even now I was determined to keep up a good front.

Josie smiled at me and handed me a tape. 'A little souvenir of today,' she said. I took it in a kind of daze.

As we were leaving Maddy cried out in her normal voice, 'I think you're mad. He's just bursting with comic talent.' As if in sympathy, her wig gave a little wiggle, and sprang forward.

Outside Serena the Sorcerer pounced on us. 'How did you—?' Then she saw my face and stepped back in horror. 'Oh no.'

I just waved a hand at her. 'Really glad you got through and I'll watch you on the telly too and cheer when you come on. I promise.'

Maddy and I stumbled our way towards reception. It might sound big-headed, but I never thought I'd lose. Not after coming so far. I felt totally humiliated. I'm obviously nowhere near as good as I think I am.

Maddy tried to say something. But I didn't want to talk to her. I didn't want to talk to anyone except ... my mum and dad. Clearly, the shock of losing must have turned my head. But at that moment, I just wanted my parents. No one else would do.

And then I thought I saw my dad come striding into reception. Is that really him, I wondered, or am I totally losing my marbles?

Suddenly this Dad look-alike spotted me and gave a remarkable impression of those toys whose eyes pop right out of their heads when you squeeze them.

'That's your dad,' hissed Maddy helpfully.

He ran over to us. He was staring at me, all shocked and anxious. 'Louis, what on earth's going on?'

I wasn't exactly sure how to answer that one but luckily, my agent, her wig now hanging right over her forehead, answered for me. 'Louis's been auditioning to be on the telly. And he would have done it too if it hadn't been for those two sleazeballs on the panel.'

Dad gaped at her. 'Maddy,' he cried incredulously. 'But why are you—?'

'I had to be accompanied by a parent,' I interrupted.

Dad still looked bewildered but all at once this tiny twinkle came into his eyes. And then another familiar figure burst into reception: Mike.

If I stood here long enough would the whole of my road turn up? Mike gave a sharp gurgle when he spotted me. 'So you found one of them,' he barked. 'But where's my boy?' He was directing that question at me. 'Theo's with you, isn't he?'

'Theo?' I looked at Dad questioningly.

'Theo has also been absent from school

today,' said Dad quietly. 'We thought he'd run off with you.'

After I'd convinced Mike that Theo wasn't hiding in my bag all four of us went over to Dad's car. Dad and Mike sat in the front, Mike spending most of the time babbling furiously into his mobile, while Dad tried to reassure him that Theo couldn't have gone far.

I was slouched in the back with Maddy. I whispered to her, 'I wonder how Dad knew where I was?' She just shrugged her shoulders. 'I suppose it doesn't really matter. It's all over now,' I said.

Dad dropped Mike off, then he took Maddy home. She'd taken off her wig and glasses and kept trying to make conversation. But I couldn't even look at her properly. I knew I'd let her down so badly. And what about all that money she'd spent on me?

'I will pay you the money back,' I announced, suddenly.

'Oh, I don't care about that,' she cried. But I bet she did.

'It might take a while, though,' I admitted, 'as I'm giving up being a comedian.'

She went all gaspy. 'Oh no, you mustn't.'

I waved a weary hand. Right now, I didn't want to talk to anyone. I just wanted to be alone with my broken dreams. As she got out of the car Maddy said, 'See you very soon.' I was too crushed with gloom to even answer her.

Back home I dreaded facing Mum, expecting a right ear-bashing, but she only said, 'Have you any idea what you've put us through today?' Amazingly, that was it, really. Of course, Elliot was gambolling about demanding to know exactly where I'd been.

And then Prue came round. There was still no news of Theo. I remembered how he'd shaken hands with me yesterday. He'd been planning to run away, hadn't he? I remembered something else too.

'I don't know if it's any use,' I piped up, 'but Theo told me once that if he ever wanted a bit of time to think things out he goes to the park and—'

'The park!' exclaimed Prue. 'We haven't looked there.' She charged out of the house, with Mum close behind.

I muttered to Dad, 'I'll just go and unpack,' as if I'd been away on holiday. But I didn't unpack or go and get my video (which I'd left in the car). I just crashed out on my bed.

Later I heard Mum come back. 'They've found Theo,' she announced to Dad. 'He was in the park, all huddled up on a bench.'

'Poor lad,' cried Dad. Then he muttered something about pressure, which I couldn't quite catch, but Mum murmured in agreement with it, anyhow. Then they both came up to see me. I snapped my eyes shut and gave a very convincing impression of someone sleeping.

'He's shattered,' said Dad.

'I know. When he came in he looked so worn out I couldn't be angry with him,' whispered Mum.

Must remember that: if ever I want to stop Mum getting cross – look tired. Then Mum discovered my running-away note, still propped up on my desk. 'Well, look at this,' she whispered.

They both read it and then Dad murmured, 'I'm off to start my career now,' and chuckled, but not in a nasty way. Shortly afterwards they crept away. They think I'm asleep now.

And that's it. I don't think I've got anything else to tell you tonight.

11.40 p.m.
Yes I have!

After my last entry I fell asleep for a few minutes. I woke to hear myself talking (a very odd sensation). I slipped downstairs and spied Mum and Dad in the sitting room watching my video. They were both really laughing. Then they spotted me and Dad exclaimed, 'But you're very funny!'

'Don't sound so amazed,' I replied.

'You've got real talent,' he said. A small smile played around his lips. 'I thought I had some musical ability when I was a teenager. And maybe I had.'

'Yes, maybe,' I said kindly.

'But I lacked something else which you've got in spades: real determination.' Then he and Mum started firing all these questions at me about the auditions. But it wasn't like one of their interrogations. They seemed incredibly interested. So I told them just about everything. Once or twice I could see Mum wanted to go all tutty but she swallowed hard and restrained herself.

We watched the tape together twice more. And they didn't seem to mind that most of my act was making fun of them. That impressed me.

Then Elliot sneaked downstairs, insisted on watching the video too, laughed loudly at all of it and then promptly fell asleep. Dad carried him upstairs while Mum plonked herself next to me on the couch. And I thought, Here it comes, the big lecture.

'When you're a parent, Louis,' she said, 'you have to play lots of different roles, like doctor, nurse, psychiatrist, friend, teacher—'

'Stop whenever you want, Mum,' I interrupted.

She smiled. 'But sometimes you can get so carried away with one part, you forget about all the others.'

The next thing I knew she'd planted one of her slurpy kisses on my forehead. But the curtains were drawn so I didn't stop her. I suddenly discovered I was starving hungry. Mum made me beans on toast and while I was chomping away Dad said, 'So you don't like us coming into your bedroom while you're working' – in this really astonished voice, as if I'd never mentioned it before!

I patiently explained to them why I didn't like being watched while I'm working, or being pressurized about school work. Also, I didn't like them organizing all my free time and neither, I added, in a rare burst of brotherly concern, did Elliot. After which I told them exactly why I hated everything about my new school, and I really felt they were listening to me. *At last*.

And I have to admit the time just flew. In fact, when Mum suddenly said, 'My goodness, it's gone eleven,' I was astonished.

The mood was now distinctly mellow. 'So have I got to go to school tomorrow?' I asked, never really expecting my dad to reply, 'No, you can have a break from the "hell-hole", as you call it, tomorrow.'

Mum looked as if she was going to disagree with Dad but then said quietly, 'All right, not tomorrow.'

When I came back up to my room I started thinking of how my dream had floated right away from me today. This plunged me right down into gloomsville again. But then I remembered my mum and dad chortling away at my video. And that did bring a tiny smile to my defeated lips.

12.15 a.m.
Just thought of something I meant to tell you earlier. I asked my dad how he knew where to find me today. He said the school had rung up about eleven o'clock to say Theo and yours truly were missing. Immediately, Prue assumed I'd abducted her precious Theo and was leading him into a life of crime and wrongdoing. Then my dad and Mike rushed back from work and there was more aggro as Mike also blamed me for leading Theo astray.

But then, at around one o'clock, they got this mysterious phone call. It was a woman's voice. She told them where I was and how I was auditioning for a top TV show, but before Dad could ask her any questions she rang off.

It must have been Josie. But why would she call my dad, especially when she thought my mum was there? That's a right puzzler.

A Surprise Re-appearance

FRIDAY MAY 17TH

12.30 p.m.
Want to hear some great news? No, the TV company hasn't rung to say they want me on the show after all. That would be beyond super or brilliant or ... anyhow, it isn't that. But it's still pretty mind-blowing.

I haven't got to go back to Spitty's Waxworks next Monday or Tuesday or Wednesday or Thursday ... or, in fact, ever again! Mum said the school and myself were clearly mismatched. She made it sound as if we were dating. She went on to say that it wasn't right that I felt so unhappy and alienated and that she and Dad were arranging for me to start at a brand new prison.

There is just one catch. While I'm between schools I will have to have a private tutor. Now, I really don't approve of bringing teachers into the home. Gruesome habit. But wait until you hear who my tutor is.

You remember they mentioned this tutor before. I thought his name was Mr Walrus, though I hadn't been listening very hard. Actually, his name is Mr Wallace. That still didn't mean anything to me until they announced his first name: Todd. Yes, Todd from Drama Club. They knew I liked him and had discovered that as well as acting in *The Bill* and coaching drama, he teaches English and basic maths. He starts next Tuesday.

5.00 p.m.
This afternoon I visited Theo. Mike opened the door. He looked red and bewildered. Theo's got some kind of chill, apparently. He keeps shivering and the doctor says he needs complete rest. Wish he'd say that about me. To be fair, Theo

didn't look the picture of health. He was dead pale and his eyes seemed to have sunk right into his head. Hated seeing him like that, actually. But, ever keen to strike a cheery note, I said, 'So we both missed the dreaded maths test, then.'

Theo just gave this sad little smile and whispered, 'Did you hear about me shouting at my parents yesterday?'

'No, but tell me everything.'

'Well, last night I'd just got back from the park, when Dad had a go at me. I'd expected that. But he went on and on about how he and Mum had poured their lifeblood into me, until something snapped inside me and I thought, I can't take any more of this. So I started screaming at them.'

'What did you say?' I asked eagerly.

'I told them to stop pouring their lifeblood into me and to leave me alone, as they were like this great, heavy weight on me and . . . and I was sick of them.'

'Oh, excellent. Say anything else?'

'No.'

'That's a shame. So what did they say?'

'Not much, just looked really shocked. But this morning Dad came and sat down on my bed and talked to me for hours. He said he was on my side and just wanted the best for me. And it was extremely important I understand that. I said I did, because he does mean well, doesn't he?'

I just shrugged my shoulders.

'I think he does,' he whispered. Then he leaned back and closed his eyes.

'I'll be off then,' I said. 'Get well soon, won't you.'

I'd just reached the door when he muttered, 'When I'm better Dad said he's arranged something special for me.'

'A trip to Disneyland?'

'No.' Theo opened his eyes again. 'A new course for children which he says is proving extremely popular. It's all about anger management.'

'Well, don't save a place for me.'

Theo started to laugh. 'Come back soon,' he said.

9.00 p.m.
I've tried to ring Maddy several times today but her mobile is permanently switched off. Hope her parents haven't confiscated it as a punishment for yesterday.

SATURDAY MAY 18TH

A leaflet for a salsa dancing class dropped through the letter box today. I placed the leaflet on the kitchen table. Dad picked it up.

'So are you going to join this time?' I asked.

'Shall we?' said Mum, looking at Dad and laughing.

'Why not,' he replied, then he started laughing too.

I really think I've found them a hobby at last. That's a big worry off my mind. Still no answer from Maddy's phone.

When Parents Are Overtrained

Just after lunch today I got an urgent call from Maddy's mum. Maddy had locked herself in her bedroom and wouldn't come out. Would I try and talk to her?

Dad drove me round and said he'd be back for me in an hour. Maddy's parents were standing waiting for me at the door. They looked really upset.

'She ran upstairs just after breakfast,' said Maddy's mum, 'and announced she wasn't coming out ever again. At first we thought she was just having a tantrum. But she won't even talk to us, and screamed the house down when I suggested getting her sisters back from a

189

friend's house. Will you try and talk to her, Louis?'

'Of course I will,' I replied. 'Can I just ask you, did you tell Maddy off for what happened on Thursday?'

They both looked puzzled. 'But what happened on Thursday?'

Oh, nothing much – your daughter skived off school, went to London and dressed up as my mum. Just a typical day, really. But clearly, they didn't know anything about that and now really wasn't the best moment to enlighten them.

On Maddy's door was a notice. It said, 'My room. My mess.'

I knocked on the door.

'What do you want?' demanded a voice.

'To see you would be nice.'

'I've got nothing to say to you,' she replied.

'Well, you can just look at me then. Come on, let me in.'

She opened the door a crack, signalled to me to come in, then bolted it shut again. She didn't look at all pleased to see me. In fact, I've had warmer welcomes from Spitty. 'What's wrong?' I asked.

She gave what I believe is called a

mirthless laugh. 'Everything,' she cried. 'I put a lot of time and effort into helping you. And then on Thursday you just brushed me aside.'

'No I didn't.'

'You did, Louis. You said it was all over and you didn't want to know me any more.'

'I never said that last bit.'

'Well, you implied it. I said, "See you very soon," and you never even answered me and I think that was extremely mean of you, especially when I dressed up as your mother and rang—' She stopped.

'What?' I asked.

'Nothing.' She was blushing madly.

And right then I knew. 'It wasn't Josie who rang my mum and dad that day, it was you, wasn't it?'

'Of course it was.'

'Why?'

'I know I told you to train your parents. But the thing is, I've overtrained mine. And I didn't want that to happen to you. So I thought, if they saw you and realized how good you were . . .'

'That was really thoughtful of you,' I said.

'Yes, it was.'

Then I asked what she meant about overtraining her parents. She sat down on her bed. 'Well, I can't talk to my parents at all now. They've never been very keen on me and I don't blame them. I mean, there are my sisters, all bright, beautiful and funny – even you fancied them.'

'No, I didn't.'

'Yes you did.'

'Excuse me, but I should know who I fancy,' I said.

'It doesn't matter,' said Maddy. 'Everyone adores them and then there's me: the ugly duckling.'

'You're not ugly,' I said, 'and you're not exactly a duckling either.'

She shook her head. 'I told myself I didn't care what my parents thought of me. I'd go my own way and keep them right out of my life. So I did all the training things I taught you. And it worked. They left me alone more and more. And they stopped expecting things from me, which is what I wanted.

'But I could see them hating me too. Only that didn't matter because along you came and I became your agent . . . but now that's all finished and I've got nothing.'

She started to cry then and I wasn't at all sure what to do. So in the end I flung a hankie at her. 'It's all right,' I said, 'it hasn't got any bogies on it.'

She smiled and blew her nose really hard. 'Sorry about that.'

'And I'm sorry I told you I'm giving up being a comedian, because I'm not—'

She looked up. 'I should think not.'

'And I'd very much like you to go on being my agent ... and my friend.' I whispered those last three words but Maddy heard me all right.

We chatted a bit longer, then I went and told Maddy's parents that she would be down any second now. Huge sighs of relief. 'Now, can I ask you a question?' I began.

'Of course,' said Maddy's dad.

'You do like Maddy, don't you?'

They both sort of jumped and chorused, 'Yes,' very indignantly.

'That's fine then,' I mumbled. 'I was just checking.'

'We love her,' went on Maddy's dad, in that same indignant voice.

'Oh, even better. That's the stuff,' I said quickly. 'Maybe you could let Maddy know that sometime. She does still want you in her life, you know.' They were both just staring at me now, no doubt drinking in my words of wisdom. 'Well, I hope that's helped. I'll call again soon. Bye.'

Feeling well chuffed with my new role as 'agony uncle', I went outside just as Dad pulled up.

Maddy was watching from her bedroom window. I signalled to her to open it.

'It's all right,' I said, 'they don't hate you, in fact . . .' But I didn't want to shout the word 'love' down the road so instead I said, 'They're pretty keen on you.'

All at once Maddy started smiling. 'You do make me laugh.'

'Well, I should do, I'm a comedian,' I said.

'And don't you ever forget it,' she called after me.

TUESDAY MAY 21ST

First lesson with Todd today. I said, 'No offence, Todd, but I am amazed to see someone who's been in *The Bill* doing a menial job like this.'

He said he was quite surprised too. He thought he'd be starring in his own hit TV series by now. (He laughed and looked mournful after he'd said that.) But he said acting is highly competitive and even the very best have periods when they're resting. That's why you need something to fall back on. He'd gone to two auditions recently and made the shortlist both times but didn't get any further.

'Don't you get discouraged?' I asked him.

'Oh yes.'

'But you still keep trying.'

'There's an old Japanese saying I've pinned up on my kitchen wall. It says, "A problem is really a mountain filled with treasure."'

I thought about this for a moment. 'Todd,' I cried, 'you've actually taught me something worth knowing today. Congratulations.'

After he'd gone Mum didn't rush up and start scrutinizing what I'd done today. There was a certain amount of hand-twitching but she restrained herself. I know she is trying very hard to conquer this bad habit. She's making excellent progress too.

Maddy rang this evening. She has found out for certain that her parents don't hate her, which is very cheering. But she is also unsure how to proceed with the parent-training. Should she just abandon all her principles?

I told her that the problem with her training programme is that parents can take what you do personally, and think you don't like them (rather than you just want a bit of a rest from them). It needs an extra ingredient, and I think I've just discovered what it is.

You find out what your parents really, really like and every so often throw them that scrap. At once, you've got something majorly important: *bargaining power*. Parent-training is a bit like snake-charming, really. Hit the right notes now and then, and you can do what you want with them. Maddy was dead impressed by my wisdom.

THURSDAY MAY 23RD

After my boasting yesterday I must admit to one failure: I still haven't got my television released back into the community. Mum and Dad are proving surprisingly stubborn on this one. I suspect they're trying to save a bit of pride. Mum keeps saying, 'No, we were right about that.' I have at least managed to get some compensation. They're buying me some CDs on Saturday.

FRIDAY JUNE 14TH

Had a look round my new school today. Also met the headmaster. Face like a beaten-up football and the most impressive collection of hairs up his nose I've ever seen. Yes, he was ugly and odd. But then they all are, aren't they? They wouldn't want the job if they weren't. But he was nowhere near as ghastly as Spitty. He was also about a hundred years younger. And the school reminded me of my old (pre-Spitty) one.

'So,' asked my dad as we were looking round it, 'do you think you could be happy here?'

Of course, the words school and happy just don't go together. But I told Dad, yeah, he could close the deal.

An Amazing Phone Call

FRIDAY JULY 5TH

5.10 p.m.

My mobile rang ten minutes ago. I thought it was Maddy. She often calls at this time. Instead, of all people, it was Josie.

I was totally shocked. And for a mad moment I thought, She's ringing to say they do want me on the show after all. And I think she realized that, because she very quickly said that the shows were all recorded and going out next week. 'I was very sorry you didn't get through,' she said. 'Among the judges it was a split decision. And. . .' she paused for a couple of seconds . . . 'the other judges didn't

198

share my sense of humour.'

'The fools,' I said.

She chuckled. 'Well, humour is a very personal thing. But I also wanted to tell you, Louis, that I'm seeing a friend of mine who's planning a different kind of talent show for children. Something with perhaps a bit more edge. Can I mention your name to him?'

'Oh yeah, sure, please do.'

'I can't promise anything. Nothing is guaranteed in this business. But I'm sure he'd like to meet you.'

'And I'd like to meet him. Thanks, Josie, thanks very much.'

Just as she was about to ring off she asked, suddenly. 'That person with you wasn't really your mother, was she?'

'No, not quite,' I admitted.

Josie started to laugh then. She was still laughing when she rang off. Talk about amazing phone calls. That's why I wanted to write it all down straight away, dear diary.

I'm on my last page for now. No space to write any more. My time is up and I must, very reluctantly, leave the stage. You've been a great audience and I'd really like to tell you one last joke but my head's still spinning from that phone call.

Just can't wait to tell my parents about it. But first of all, I'm going to call my agent.

Smile on!

Louis the Laugh.

Some things you may not know about Pete Johnson:

- He used to be a film critic on Radio One. Sometimes he saw three films a day.

- He has met a number of famous actors and directors, and collects signed film pictures.

- Pete's favourite book when he was younger was *One Hundred and One Dalmations*. Pete wrote to the author of this book, Dodie Smith. She was the first person to encourage Pete to be a writer. *Traitor* is dedicated to her.

- Once when Pete went to a television studio to talk about his books he was mistaken for an actor and taken to the audition room. TV presenter Sarah Greene also once mistook Pete for her brother.

- When he was younger Pete used to sleepwalk regularly. One night he woke up to find himself walking along a busy road in his pyjamas.

- Pete's favourite food is chocolate. He especially loves Easter eggs and received over forty this year.

- Pete's favourites of his own books are *The Ghost Dog* and *How to Train Your Parents*. The books he enjoys reading most are thrillers and comedies.

- Pete likes to start writing by eight o'clock in the morning. He reads all the dialogue aloud to see if it sounds natural. When he's stuck for an idea he goes for a long walk.

- He carries a notebook wherever he goes. 'The best ideas come when you're least expecting them' he says.

- And he collects jokes!

[You've sent me some brilliant ones. On the next page are a few of my favourites...]

What's the difference between
bogies and broccoli?
Children don't eat broccoli.
Matthew, Southend-on-Sea

What's faster, heat or cold?
Heat – you can catch a cold.
Hayley, Omagh

Doctor, I keep seeing the future.
When did this happen?
Next Tuesday.
David, Prestatyn

A man rings up an airport and asks how long it
takes to fly from London to Spain.
'Just a minute,' says the girl.
'Wow, that's fast,' cries the man.
Gary, Kettering

My grandad was a pianist on the Titanic.
He went down very well.
Zeenat, Acton

What do you call a rich rabbit?
A million hare.
Rebecca, Holmer Green

What happened to the man who
stole a calendar?
He got twelve months.
Mohammed, Luton

RESCUING DAD
Pete Johnson

How do you improve your dad?

Joe and Claire can see why Mum chucked
Dad out. He looks a mess, he can't cook and
he's useless around the house. Something
must be done: they're the only ones who can
help transform him into 'Dad Mark Two'.
And when they unveil this new, improved
dad, Mum will be so impressed she'll take
him back on the spot!

But then disaster strikes – Mum starts seeing the slimy and creepy Roger. And Joe and
Claire's plans take an unexpected turn –
with hilarious results.

'Pete Johnson is a wonderful story-teller'
Evening Standard

ISBN 0 440 864577

TRAITOR
Pete Johnson

*Have the bullies pushed
someone too far?*

What would *you* do if a gang of bullies
decided to waylay you on your way home
from school, demanding money?
Would you pay up?

That's what Tom, Mia and Oliver do – at
first. Ashamed of being victims, united in
their fear of the gang, they feel powerless to
do anything else. But as the pressure
builds more and more, a terrible suspicion
begins to surface: could one of the three
friends be *helping* the bullies? And if so,
just who is... the traitor?

A perceptive and highly credible tale of
bullying and friendship from award-
winning Pete Johnson, author of *The Ghost
Dog, Rescuing Dad* and many other titles.

ISBN 0 440 864380

MY FRIEND'S A WEREWOLF
Pete Johnson

*Now I know for certain Simon
is a werewolf!*

Kelly always thought werewolves only
existed in stories and late-night films.
Until Simon moves in next door. Kelly and
Simon become instant friends, but Kelly
just can't help noticing that there's something very odd about her new friend. For
one thing, he wears black gloves all the
time – even at school. And could that be
hair starting to sprout on his face? Last,
but definitely not least, there's the howling
at night...

Aren't werewolves... dangerous?

CORGI YEARLING BOOKS

ISBN 0 440 863422